The Devil Wears
Baccarat 2

Jatoria C.

The Devil Wears Baccarat 2

Copyright © 2024 by Jatoria C.

All rights reserved.

Published in the United States of America.

All rights reserved. No part of this publication may be reproduced, distributed, or transmitted in any form or by any means, including photocopying, recording, or other electronic or mechanical methods, without the prior written permission of the publisher, except in the case of brief quotations embodied in critical reviews and certain other noncommercial uses permitted by copyright law. For permission requests, please contact: www.colehartsignature.com

This is a work of fiction. Names, characters, places, and incidents either are the products of the author's imagination or are used fictitiously. Any resemblance of actual persons, living or dead, businesses, companies, events, or locales is entirely coincidental. The publisher does not have any control and does not assume any responsibility for author or third-party websites or their content.

The unauthorized reproduction or distribution of this copyrighted work is a crime punishable by law. No part of the book may be scanned, uploaded to or downloaded from file sharing sites, or distributed in any other way via the Internet or any other means, electronic, or print, without the publisher's permission. Criminal copyright infringement, including infringement without monetary gain, is investigated by the FBI and is punishable by up to five years in federal prison and a fine of $250,000 (www.fbi.gov/ipr/).

This book is licensed for your personal enjoyment only. Thank you for respecting the author's work.

Published by Cole Hart Signature, LLC.

Mailing List

To stay up to date on new releases, plus get information on contests, sneak peeks, and more,

Go To The Website Below...

www.colehartsignature.com

Message to the Readers:

Hey, guys, before you go any further, it's important that you read this part. This is a DARK romance. It includes themes such as graphic violence, profanity, explicit sexual situations, non/con dub, mental health issues, and abuse. Please take this warning seriously and proceed with caution. I love you guys 🫶

Where we left off
Constatin

The Mind was what my father called me. I was supposed to be the smart one, the one who figured everything out. Where the fuck was my mind when my best friend was plotting against me? Where the fuck was my mind when the head of our security was planning to kill us? I took a sip of my liquor before glancing around at my brother's wedding. Everybody was on the dance floor, having an enjoyable time. I had even seen my mother smile once or twice today.

On the outside looking in, one would assume I was handling everything going on in my normal cool, calculated way. My brothers and I were taught at an early age how to conceal our true emotions from showing on our faces. So, although I may have outwardly appeared calm, cool, and in control, I was really boiling with rage inside.

All day, I could feel people's eyes on me, and it was to be expected as the Nasu or the Godfather of the Romanian Mafia. My brother had some of the biggest mafia families in attendance today, and I knew they all wondered what my next move would be. The people I trusted the most had betrayed me in the worst way, and I had to set an example that would be remembered for generations to come.

Before I could plot my revenge, though, I needed to get married and fast. I was only given sixty days to find a new bride, and thirty of those days had already passed. To be honest, it did not matter to me who I married. The marriage would be a business transaction for me and nothing more. My eyes went back to the dance floor, and I saw my brother's new wife, Kenya, dancing with her best friend. I believe her name was Ari. They were complete opposites of each other. Kenya was taller than her and slim, with a dark-chocolate skin complexion. Her best friend could not be more than five feet tall. She had what my mama called baby-making hips, and her skin complexion was almost peanut butter colored.

"Fiul (son)," my mama called out to me from the dance floor.

She wanted me to come dance with her, but there was no way I was going out there on the dance floor with this aggravating ass cane. I had two more weeks of physical therapy before I could ditch it. The doctor said that I would always walk with a slight limp, but eventually, it would be barely noticeable. Flashbacks of my best friend shooting a bullet through my knee appeared in my mind again. Elizabeth was smart to run and hide. She knew, like I knew, that her days of being alive would end soon.

An hour later, I stood up from the table where I sat to wish my brother and his new wife farewell on their honeymoon. I grabbed my cane to walk to the bathroom to relieve my bladder. My security guards followed closely behind me. When I reached the bathroom, they went in before me to clear the bathroom stalls. Unfortunately, being the head of the Romanian Mafia came with having a lot of enemies, known and unknown.

I leaned against the wall, waiting for my security guards to finish the bathroom check, when someone bumped into me from behind. My cane slipped out of my hand and onto the floor. I felt wet liquid on my charcoal-colored suit jacket. I grabbed my gun from my waist and turned around.

"Oh, my god! Please don't shoot me. Shit, y'all motherfuckers are crazy," Kenya's best friend said before reaching down to pick up my cane. Her voice had a slight slur to it.

Alexandur and Kenya had two open bars for their guests at the wedding. Judging from the way her light brown skin appeared flushed and the slight slur to her words, she had to have partaken in the open bar's alcoholic beverages more than a few times.

"Here. My bad. Also, I accidentally spilled my cup on your jacket. If you send me the bill from the cleaners, I will pay it," she said.

I turned my head to the side and studied her more. She was a beautiful woman. All the women I have dated in the past were either average height or tall due to my large, prodigious frame, but I found Ari's miniature size compelling.

"Um, excuse me, *Mr. Man with the Gun*, are you going to get your cane from my hand or continue looking at me crazy?"

Ari reached her hand out to hand me my cane again, but I did not reach out to retrieve it from her.

"Sir, can you stop staring at me like that? It was an accident. I already apologized. What more do you want?"

Now, her voice was full of attitude, and I found it amusing.

I just found the solution to my problem.

"That is a good question, Ari. Because what I want is your hand in marriage and a baby. Unfortunately for you, I am not giving you a choice in the matter."

"Excuse me! What?!" she yelled in disbelief.

Her eyes had squinted, and she was staring at me as if I were an alien or some other unknown species that she was seeing for the first time in her life.

"I do not like to repeat myself. As my wife, it would be best for you to learn this lesson now instead of later."

"Are you joking, or do you really believe the bullshit coming out of your mouth?"

"Jokes are for comedians and a comedian, I am not. I am the Nasu. Nothing I say should be taken as a joking matter," I replied blankly.

"Look, crazy man, I don't know what the hell is wrong with you, nor do I care. The best advice I can give you is if you are experiencing any alarming medical symptoms as a result of a recent or past incident, it would be best for you to seek professional medical help at once. Head injuries are dangerous and can be life-threatening if not taken seriously."

Ari no longer looked shocked but concerned.

That is right. Alexander did mention something about her moving here to work as a nurse.

My lips spread slightly, and for the first time in weeks, I almost smiled.

"There is not anything wrong with my head. I am of sound mind. You and I will be getting married, as I previously stated."

Ari's eyes got big, and she opened her mouth to respond but was distracted by my security guards walking out of the bathroom.

"All clear, sir," Emet said from behind me.

Ari leaned my cane against the wall and turned around to walk away without saying another word. For her to be so small in stature, she moved her legs rapidly away from me and back to the dance floor. Briefly, I wondered if she would continue dancing, but instead, she walked to the table where she was sitting and picked up her purse. Ari then reached down to give my mother a quick hug and waved goodbye to all the other people sitting at the table before walking toward the exit.

She has a good intuition. Leaving was the smartest thing she could do. Sadly, it would only going to give her a false sense of security.

One

Two weeks later

The steaming hot coffee burned my lips as I lifted the brown coffee mug my secretary handed to me fifteen minutes ago when I entered my office floor. The burning pain was a nice welcome, even if it was only a fleeting sensation. In front of my office desk stood Alexandur, Roman, and Kofi. Alexandur and Kenya had returned from their honeymoon a little after seven this morning. After they landed, Alexandur and Kenya drove home, only to be greeted by police officers waiting for them outside their residence.

"Calm down and tell me what the officers said verbatim," I demanded.

Alexandur closed his eyes and took a few deep breaths. He was dressed down in an alabaster white button-down shirt with matching alabaster white pants. Alexandur was not scheduled to return to work until tomorrow to give him and Kenya time to get their affairs in order at home after being gone across the country for the last couple of weeks. I could tell the monster inside of him was fighting to come out, and I had plans today that did not involve watching my brother butchering police officers to death. Fifteen seconds passed before he opened his eyes again, and I could see the monster in his eyes had faded to some degree.

"When I pulled up to my gate, there was a police cruiser parked in front of it. I told Kenya to stay in the car so I could see what the hell they wanted. When I got out of my car, the two officers sitting in the police cruiser followed suit and exited their vehicle. I leaned against the door of my car and watched them as they approached me. It was clear to see that they were upset about something. They both were frowning and looking at me with anger. Obviously, whoever had sent them to my home did not inform them to tread lightly, especially in front of my beautiful wife. The officers introduced themselves when they reached me. They were both Caucasian, but one was a male and the other a female. The blond male was introduced as Mr. Gram, and the brunette-haired woman was Mrs. Knight."

Alexandur's eyes started to darken again, and his fingers clenched tightly into fists. My eyes went from him to Kofi. Kofi is Kenya's little brother and our newly hired information consultant. He was no longer standing in front of my desk but was now sitting on my black leather couch with his laptop out, typing away. My eyes went from him over to Roman. Roman still stood next to Alexandur, but he did not appear interested in the conversation we were having. His eyes were staring straight ahead, not looking at anything.

"What was the reason for Mr. Gram and Mrs. Knight's visit?" I asked Alexandur after returning my gaze to him.

"Apparently, there were two dead bodies found this morning, and I am a person of interest."

Alexandur smirked briefly before continuing his story.

"Some sick bastard left Steven Hall and Quan Miller's dead bodies on the police chief's lawn this morning. Not only were they killed, but their bodies were set on fire."

This is intriguing. The police chief was only still alive because my father was dead. The last couple of months have been hectic, and my focus has been elsewhere. I will have to make time to visit the police chief sooner rather than later.

"After they informed me of that news, Officer Gram asked me about my whereabouts around five and six this morning. Apparently, that is the time the dead officers' bodies were dumped on the police chief's lawn to be discovered. I informed him that we had just returned home from our honeymoon. He asked which airline we flew on and what time we landed. I laughed before turning around to walk away."

"Do I need to get one of your lawyers to reach out to the officers on the case to provide evidence that Alexandur and my sister were 30,000 feet in the air during that time and could not have committed the murders?" Kofi interrupted to ask me.

"Yes, and find the location of the police chief too. He had to be the one to point the officers in Alexandur's direction," I replied before leaning back in my office chair.

Kofi continued typing away on his laptop.

"The only people who knew about Kenya's arrest are us and whoever you involved in the clean-up," I told Alexandur.

"I have personally spoken with that individual and can confirm they have no inkling about the police officers' murders, nor were they involved."

Alexandur shook his head when he spoke, and it was clear from the tone of his voice that he was positive about this information.

Well, who in the Hell killed the officers, then?

I stood up from my desk and leaned my hands down on top of it. My knee ached slightly, but I had become accustomed to the feeling. It had only been a couple of days since the doctor cleared me to walk without my cane. I still had a slight limp when I walked, but there was nothing I could do about it.

"Kofi, did you do it?" I asked.

Kofi stopped typing and looked up at me. He smiled and then shook his head. Kofi had been training in sharp shooting and hand-to-hand combat. He was more than capable of killing anybody if he had the desire to do so. My eyes went to my little brother Roman.

"Did you do it, Roman?" I asked him.

Roman did not even glance at me. Silence filled the room, and I waited patiently for a response. A couple of minutes passed before my anger began to rise.

"Roman, answer my damn question!" I ordered.

Roman had been even quieter and to himself since our father was murdered. Alexandur had told me at his wedding that he was worried about him, but I brushed it off.

A couple more seconds passed before my little brother finally spoke.

"Can I go? Mother wants me to take her shopping this morning, and I do not want to be late," he replied.

Kofi stopped typing again and looked at Roman like he was out of his mind. Clearly, something was wrong with him. Not only am I his older brother, but I am his Nasu. Anybody else would have been killed for ignoring my direct order. The urge to choke the answers out of him hit me, but I had plans, and I disliked not sticking to my plans.

I gave Roman a warning look, which he pretended not to see, before removing my suit jacket.

"Brother, had me your knife," I told Alexandur.

Alexandur frowned but reached inside his jacket to remove the knife he kept hidden under his clothes. While I waited, I rolled the right sleeve of my shirt all the way up to the top of my arm. Alexandur handed me the knife, and I stabbed myself in the center of my arm and then sliced down four inches from the puncture wound. The knife went in deep enough that it would require medical attention but not deep enough to cause damage to any major arteries that could result in my death.

"What the fuck?" I heard Kofi mumble.

I wiped the blood on my white shirt to clean it off before handing the knife back to Alexandur.

"Brother, what is this?" Alexandur asked me.

"Today is the day I visit my wife. I will be back in a few hours," I replied.

Alexandur's eyes widened, and I knew he wanted to object. Ari had called Kenya on her honeymoon and told her about our conversation. Alexandur had called me and asked me if I could reconsider my decision and choose another wife, but my mind was made up. Blood had begun to drip down my suit jacket and onto my office desk. My jaw clenched, looking at the mess, but I would get my secretary to wipe it up while I was gone. As my brothers exited my office, I reached into my desk drawer to pull out a large white handkerchief with my left hand and make a quick tourniquet on my right arm.

Alexandur was clearly concerned, but he knew questioning me any further would be a sign of disrespect. After the tourniquet was on my arm, I walked around my office desk and to the door. My security guards, Emet and Mikey, were standing outside my office.

"Come on," I told them as I closed and locked my office door.

Ari

My alarm sounded off, waking me from my sleep. Slowly, I opened both my eyes and let them adjust to the sunlight peering into my bedroom from the window. My right hand came from up under my burgundy bedding set and hit the top of my alarm clock to silence it.

In today's society, most people just used their phones as an alarm, but I preferred using an old-school alarm clock to wake me up. When I first started college, I tried using the alarm on my phone, but I kept falling asleep without putting it on the charger. The next day, I would wake up well-rested but late as hell for classes.

Minutes passed while I lay still in bed, just staring off into space before I forced myself to get up. I sat up in bed and stretched my arms out wide. Kenya was kind enough to reach out to her landlord and ask if she could sign her lease over to me when I informed her that I planned to move here. She had still been paying the bills for the two-bedroom house she lived in before she met Alexandur because she didn't want to break her lease agreement. Luckily, the landlord agreed, and I didn't have to stay in a hotel while I searched for a place to live.

The time on the clock now read seven seventeen in the morning, and I groaned. My shift at work started at 8:30, and if I didn't get out of bed now, I would be late.

Today was my fourth day working at Emory University Hospital, and it had been a whirlwind. Interning taught me a lot, but nothing could have prepared me for working as a trauma nurse in the emergency department at the hospital. The first two days, I came home and cried myself to sleep. There were so many patients with stabbing or shooting wounds that I experienced my first death within three hours of working on my first day. I wish I could say the death rate had slowed down, but unfortunately, Atlanta is completely different from Tuscaloosa, Alabama, where I attended college.

The other nurses on the unit applauded me for making it through my first day without throwing up and crying. If only they knew how bad I sobbed when I made it home. Slowly, I climbed out of my bed and made it up. Five minutes later, I was in the shower. Today, Kenya returned home from her honeymoon. We had spoken several times over the last couple of weeks, but the conversations only lasted a few minutes. Kenya didn't want to tell me she was worried about me, but we had been best friends forever. Ever since I told her about the conversation I had with Alexandur's crazy ass brother, the first thing she would ask me when we got on the phone was if I was okay. I told her the other day to stop worrying so much, and it was obvious he was just terrible at telling jokes. She didn't agree, but as soon as I started questioning her about Constatin, she would change the subject instantaneously.

My thoughts drifted back to the wedding day. Constatin was a very handsome man. He was over six feet tall. His shoulders were wide like a professional linebacker in the national football league, and his muscles were so defined that they were easy to see through his clothes. His eyes were the color of aged whiskey, and his cheekbones looked so sharp that I believed I would get a papercut if I rubbed my finger across them. The smell of the cologne floating from his body was potent enough to make a lesbian weak in the knees from its peculiar scent. Constatin might have been insane in the brain, but the man was rich, fine, and had the aura of a boss. Even with the cane he was using to aid him with walking, he was still the hottest man at the wedding, in my opinion.

Stop thinking about that crazy ass man before you think him up!

My eyes shut, and I let the hot water cascade over my body for a couple of minutes after washing before opening them back and shutting off the shower. I spent the next thirty minutes finishing my morning hygiene routine, putting on my scrubs, and applying a quick lipliner and lip gloss combination to my lips. At five minutes after eight, I rushed out of the house and into my white 2020 Honda Civic.

The drive to the hospital was more like a Nascar race. The people in Atlanta drove like bats out of hell. My first time driving on the interstate almost made me have a severe panic attack. Now, I am a professional and sped through traffic, switching lanes, just like every driver in Atlanta.

The emergency room was busy. Nurses and doctors were walking swiftly to handle the patients in the twenty-eight emergency rooms we had in the back and the patients needing to be seen in the emergency room lobby. I clocked in two minutes after my shift was scheduled to start and then walked to the nurse's room to look at the white board and see what rooms I would be assigned today. After I memorized the room numbers, I found the nurse I was relieving to get the shift change notes before doing my first patient round.

Time moved by quickly, and before I knew it, I was informed

by my charge nurse that I had fifteen minutes to eat something quick before I was needed back out on the floor. I didn't like to eat heavily during the daytime. Food made me lazy, and I moved slower, accomplishing fewer tasks than I intended.

In the break room, I put a bag of Movie Theater Butter popcorn into the microwave, grabbed myself a water bottle from the employee refrigerator, and sat down at the table. My feet were aching slightly, and I made a mental note to upgrade the quality of my tennis shoes with my first check. The popcorn only took a couple of minutes to make. I got up from the table to get it before sitting back down.

While I ate and drank my water, I scrolled through TikTok. TikTok videos had me in a chokehold. Most nights, I would be in bed, watching TikTok videos, instead of sleeping like I was supposed to be. After I threw away my empty popcorn bag and water bottle, I decided to use the last few minutes to call home and check on my mother.

As I expected, my mother was still in bed resting when I called. She worked third shift as a nurse at a local nursing home. We spoke for a few minutes before I told her I had to go and promised to call her later to check back in with her. A feeling of guilt hit my body when I hung up my cell phone. My mother was now all alone, and it ate me up inside. Logically, I knew I had made the best decision by moving here. Emory Hospital paid more than any of the hospitals back home in Alabama, and they gave me a five-thousand-dollar sign-on bonus. As much as I didn't want to leave my mother alone to work and live in Atlanta, it was the best decision. Thoughts of my father invaded my mind, but I quickly pushed them away. Now wasn't the time to think about my fucked up personal life.

I got back up to wash my hands before walking out of the nurse's break room and back onto the emergency room floor.

"Mrs. Taylor," the charge nurse called my name from behind the nurse's station.

"Yes, ma'am?" I replied as I approached her.

"You have been requested in room thirteen for some sutures. The patient is a close friend of Mr. Legend. Go there immediately after signing your first and last name everywhere I point."

Mr. Legend is the CEO of the hospital. I haven't even met the guy. Who in the world is his friend?

Confused, I did as she asked. There were only a few papers that required my signature, so I quickly scribbled my name. Before I could ask the charge nurse any more questions, she had already walked away.

Frowning, I headed toward room thirteen. When I made it to the room, I put a smile on my face before knocking.

"Come in," a deep voice yelled out.

No way. It can't be.

I entered the patient's room and paused. Sitting on the hospital bed with blood all over his white collared shirt was Constatin. We stared at each other before the people standing behind him caught my eye. He had the same two security guards who were with him at the wedding. He called one of them Emet. They were similar in appearance but were Caucasian men and around six feet tall. They both had chestnut brown hair cut short close to their head. The only difference was one of them had blue eyes, and the other had dark grey eyes.

Do your job, girl. Don't let Mr. Crazy man get you in trouble.

"Good afternoon. I am Ms. Taylor, and I will be your nurse today," I spoke in the most cheerful tone that I could produce.

"Bucur. Your last name is Bucur," Constatin replied.

Yup, still crazy in the head, I see.

"Is it okay if I remove the jacket from your arm so I can see the wound?"

He smirked and nodded. The scent of his cologne made me squeeze my legs tight as I approached him. It really was not fair for him to look and smell so good. Gently, I untied the jacket from around his right arm and set it to the side.

"If you don't mind me asking, how did you get injured?" I asked.

Constatin had a stab wound going horizontally down the center of his arm that appeared to be new. It was bleeding profusely, and I was amazed that he wasn't showing any signs of distress. There was no way the wound didn't cause his body some kind of pain.

"I cut myself," he replied nonchalantly.

My hand froze on his arm, and I peered into his eyes to see if they were dilated. They weren't dilated at all, and he looked to be quite serious.

"You are terrible at telling jokes, Mr. Bucur. Can you tell me your pain level on a scale from one to ten? One being the least amount of pain, and ten being the worst."

"Ari, have I not already informed you that I do not joke. You are my wife. I will only say what I mean and mean what I say when speaking to you. The wound on my arm came from my brother's knife. I asked him to see it so I could cut myself. How else would I have seen you at work if I did not have an injury? If I had shown up and asked for your time, you would have denied me and used work as an excuse. My time is too valuable for childish games."

Silence. The room went silent after he replied because I couldn't believe the words that had just come out of his mouth. Minutes passed before I was able to regain my composure.

Girl, just stitch this crazy ass man up and get the hell away from him.

"In order to stitch this wound back up, I am going to first give you a shot to numb the area. Your arm will be sore afterward, but I will put in a request for the doctor to prescribe you some antibiotics and pain medicine," I stated as I checked his vital signs.

"I am a busy man, and I have another important matter to attend to. The shot is not necessary, nor are the prescriptions. I know how to take care of my own stab wound."

Don't say anything. Don't do it, Ari.

The urge to curse this crazy ass man out and then call up to the mental health floor to get a psychiatrist down here to admit his ass had me biting down hard on my bottom lip. Instead of responding, I turned around and walked over to the supply closet in the room to get the tools I needed.

In all honesty, I couldn't force him to accept the numbing agent or to take the medicine that I still planned to prescribe him. If Constatin showed any signs of distress, I would stop and try to convince him to be rational. Over the next fifteen minutes, I worked in silence. Constatin sat there while I cleaned the wound and stitched it up without moving. He didn't make any signs or noises of distress. The man didn't even squirm; he just sat still and let me work on him.

"Okay, Mr. Bucur, you are all stitched up. I will be back shortly with discharge papers that include instructions on proper wound care. There will also be two medical prescriptions in the packet. It will be up to you if you use them or not," I informed him while hastily cleaning up and removing my gloves.

"Let's go," he said to his security guards as he stood.

Shocked, I watched as Constatin rolled his shirt sleeve back down and started walking toward the door.

"See you later tonight, Mrs. Bucur," Constatin stated before opening the hospital room door and walking out.

Constatin

Ari stared at me in shock as I exited the hospital room. She had done a respectable job applying sutures to my arm. A part of me expected her to be shaking in fear from being so close to me. In her mind, I am just a crazy man with a limp who has nothing better to do than to spew useless words for entertainment.

Over the last couple of weeks, I had learned everything I could about her. She worked hard during her time in school and mostly maintained an A/B average in her studies, even during nursing school. Her being a quick learner and thinker will be beneficial to our marriage. The quicker she learned that I chose every syllable that I spoke carefully, she would not have to waste mental energy wondering what was going to happen next.

In the emergency room lobby, I walked to the elevators instead of outside, where Emet had parked the car. My security guards and I waited for the elevator to open and for the occupants to exit before walking inside. There were other people standing behind us, waiting to get on the elevator, but Mikey held his hand out to stop them while Emet pushed the button for the top floor.

When we reached the top floor, we exited the elevator and walked to the secretary's desk. The top floor of the hospital looked nothing like the rest of the hospital. In fact, if I had not just left the emergency room, I would not even believe I was inside the hospital.

"Hey, how can I help you today?" the secretary asked.

"I have a meeting with Mr. Legend. Tell him Mr. Bucur is here. He is expecting me."

The secretary frowned before typing a few buttons on her computer. A few moments passed, and then she picked up the phone and called who I assumed was Mr. Legend. The secretary told him that I was there, but I was not on his schedule. The call ended a few seconds later.

"Sorry about that wait. Mr. Legend's office is the second door on the right. You all can go ahead."

The secretary's voice was no longer friendly but curious. Whatever Mr. Legend said on the phone had her eyeing all three of us suspiciously. Without giving her another thought, I turned toward the direction she pointed in.

My security guards got in front of me and walked to the room she directed us to. Emet and Mikey had been my security guards for years, but after the betrayal of the other security guards and my position in the mafia changed, they took extreme security measures everywhere we went. Emet knocked on the thick mahogany wood door when we reached it.

"Come on in, gentlemen," Mr. Legend said after opening and holding his office door for us to enter.

The smell of cleaning supplies and Killian Dark Lord Cologne greeted me as I walked inside the office. Killian Dark Lord was once one of my top cologne choices before my brothers and I started paying François for our own personalized Baccarat scent. Mr. Legend pointed to the chair in front of his desk before walking around the desk to have a seat in the chair behind it.

"Did you do it?" I asked as I took the suggested seat.

Mr. Legend's nose flared, but he nodded his head in response. Jersey Legend was an honorable man from the intel I gathered. He graduated as the valedictorian of his high school and received over a million dollars in scholarship money, which he used to put himself through college to become a heart surgeon. Mr. Legend was an exceptional heart surgeon with a ninety-five percent success rate for open heart surgeries. In just seven years, he was offered the job of CEO, and he decided to put his doctor hat up and take the position.

"Here." He picked up a few papers and handed them to me.

Quickly, I scanned each document and made sure each spot was signed correctly, as I had requested. Satisfied, I folded the documents and slid them inside my suit jacket pocket. My arm was starting to sting a little, but this wasn't my first time dealing with a stab wound, and in my line of work, it would not be the last.

Now, my wife can be the one to stitch and patch up any injuries that did not require severe medical attention.

"Threatening the life of my wife was disgusting, and I hope to never have to lay eyes on any of you again."

Mr. Legend had finally dropped the polite act and let his aggression out. Everyone has a weakness, and his was his wife. When I left my home yesterday morning, I followed Mr. Legend's wife to her veterinary office. When she got out of the car, I snapped a few pictures on my cellphone.

Mr. legend stopped every morning to get coffee and read the paper at the coffee shop down the street. When he stopped yesterday, I approached him and had a seat at his coffee table. He recognized me at once and was happy that I stopped to converse with him. My family donates a couple million every year to several hospitals in Atlanta, and Emory was one of them. To his dismay, I did not stop to speak with him about a donation. It was a short conversation. He was given simple instructions to follow, and if he did not, his wife would pay the price.

Mr. Legend was an intelligent man. It did not take him long to figure out that I was not just the CEO of Bucur Wine International. Most people sensed danger; they just did not react to it until it was too late to get to safety. He spat out a few words about if anybody found out, he could lose everything he'd worked for.

Life was all about choices, and he had sixty seconds to make his. As expected, he agreed to do as I asked, and I took out the same documents that I had just folded into my suit pocket and handed them to him. Before I left, I warned him that it would be a waste of his time and mine to involve law enforcement. Half the police force was crooked, and I would know everything he reported before he left the precinct.

"Ahemmmm." Mr. Legend rudely cleared his throat, disrupting my thoughts.

"Enjoy the rest of your day," I said and stood up to leave.

There were a couple more places I needed to visit before I went back to work. It was close to lunch time when I made it back onto my floor and to my office. Kofi was in his office, next door to mine, eating pizza.

"Stay here," I told my security guards before entering Kofi's office and closing the door.

"Did you file the paperwork at the probate office?" Kofi asked me.

In his office, he had a brown leather sectional for his guests. I had a seat there before answering his question.

"Yes, I did. The official document will be mailed out in the next few weeks, but the clerk we paid to put the documents through without Ari's presence is hastening them."

"Congratulations. How does it feel being a married man?" he asked, grinning.

"It is business, nothing more. Any news with the mayor?"

"Elizabeth has not reached out to her father yet, but when she does, I will let you know asap. Wherever she and Tom are, they are being extremely careful. They are using aliases and have not used any of their credit cards."

Elizabeth's mother died from a stroke a few years ago. Her father was the only family member left that she cared about. She was daddy's princess. He spoiled her from the time she was born. It would not be long before she caved and tried to make some kind of contact with him. Once she makes contact with him, he will pay for the sins of his daughter.

"Is there anything else important that we need to discuss?" I asked Kofi.

Now that I am a married man, I need to call Mr. Vincent on the board to let them know one of my requirements as the Nasu was completed.

"Yes, there is one more thing. This morning, after I sent the lawyers to handle the incident with Alexandur, I searched for information on the police chief like you asked. As of this morning, his name is listed as being off on a two-week vacation," he replied.

"He knows there will be consequences for sending the police to Alexandur's house. As soon as you get a location on him let me know."

"Yes, sir," Kofi replied before picking up another slice of pizza and eating it.

Kofi was gaining muscles at a rapid pace from all the training he was doing. He still had a nerdy appearance, but his body was no longer long without muscle definition. *It was time to advance to the next level of his training*, I thought as I exited his office.

Ari

I watched a five-year-old child die today.

The same thought kept repeating over and over in my mind while I walked through the employee parking lot at the hospital. For the last week, every day before I left home for work, I would tell myself that there was no way I could experience anything more traumatic than what I had already experienced on my first few days on the job. God, I was so naïve.

In nursing school, we were told to focus on the lives we saved and not on the lives we couldn't save. That's easy to say, but how do I lie in bed at night and not think about an innocent child getting shot at a birthday party and dying within minutes of being wheeled into the hospital? A sob wanted to escape from my mouth, but I put my hand right over it to hold it in.

My stomach growled in hunger, but the idea of trying to eat after the horrible day I had made me want to vomit.

Calm down. You are off for the next three days. You can recharge and come back to work ready to save lives again.

I opened my car door and got inside it. My eyes shut, and I could feel tears falling down my face. Instead of trying to fight them, I just let them flow. I don't know how long I sat in the employee parking lot, silently crying, but by the time I cranked my car up to go home, I felt a little better.

The majority of the nurses and doctors at the hospital worked twelve-hour shifts. Twelve-hour shifts were tough, but it allowed for a four-day on and three-days off weekly schedule. Nurses were given one week of mandatory on-call duty every month, and this wasn't my on-call week.

For the next three days, I didn't want to do anything but curl up in my bed and watch one of my favorite TV shows. The drive to the house was a quiet one. Music was calming to my soul, but I was too exhausted mentally and physically to turn any music on.

When I finally pulled into my driveway, some of the tension in my shoulders began to relax. I got out of my car and grabbed my purse. The walk from my car to the front door only took a couple of minutes. I slid my key into the door and unlocked it.

Is that food I smell?

The aroma of food drifted to my nose, and my stomach growled again, this time loudly.

Where the fuck is that smell coming from? Oh, God. I am officially losing my damn mind.

I locked the front door and slowly walked to the kitchen. The kitchen light was on, causing me to frown.

Girl, don't take your ass in that kitchen without a weapon or something!

My thoughts were trying to warn me that danger was ahead,

but my feet didn't get the memo. I entered the kitchen and screamed.

"How the fuck did you get in here?" I yelled at Constatin's crazy ass. He was sitting at the kitchen table, scrolling on his phone, with a brown paper bag of food in front of him. He had on a new suit that wasn't covered in his own blood.

I am filing a restraining order on his ass first thing in the morning.

"Stop being so dramatic. Come sit down and have dinner with me. We have a few things to discuss."

This man had to have been dropped on his head as a baby.

"I'm calling the police."

I walked over to the counter to put my purse down so I could dig inside it for my cell phone.

"Unless we are having a domestic dispute, the police officers will not intervene in a simple marital disagreement," he replied.

"We have to be married for it to be a marital disagreement, crazy man," I mumbled, pulling my phone out of my purse.

"We are married, and I have the documents to prove it."

"Bullshit."

I turned away from the counter to watch him pull out some papers from his suit pocket.

"Ari, I am being patient with you because I know things are happening rapidly, but I will not tell you again that I do not like to waste my words or time. Disobedience will not be tolerated in this marriage. Come sit down so we can eat dinner, and I will answer every question you have.

Curiosity got the best of me. The need to prove this crazy ass man wrong was stronger than my common sense. I kept my cellphone in my hand while I walked to the kitchen table and took the seat across from him. Constatin opened the brown paper bag of food and pulled out two white takeout plates. He placed one in front of me and the other in front of himself.

Is that tacos?

My mouth watered, and I rushed to open the takeout box. In

the box were four tacos, fully loaded just how I like them, with a cup of limes on the side.

"Did you get tacos because they are my favorite?" I asked him.

"Yes."

"How in the hell do you know what my favorite food is?"

Run, girl. Runnnnnn!

"I did a full background check on you. You also have several pictures on Facebook and Instagram of you eating tacos. Well, you had. I deleted all of your social media profiles."

And just like that, my appetite was gone again.

"There is so much wrong with what you just said that I don't even know where to begin."

"Ari, ask your questions and eat. I ran you a bath, and I do not want your water to get cold."

I knocked the whole plate of takeout food onto the floor.

"What the fuck is wrong with you?" he angrily asked.

He didn't raise his voice, but it was clear from his tone that he was upset.

"No, what the fuck is wrong with you? You are insane in the brain! But I will be filing a restraining order against your crazy ass first thing in the morning!"

"We have only been married for one day, and you have done nothing but behave like a child," he said.

"Crazy. Man. We. Are. Not. Fucking. Married!" I screamed so loudly that I wouldn't have been surprised if the neighbors heard me.

Constatin took a deep breath and then tossed the folded documents to me. I unfolded the documents while he picked up a taco and took a bite. The first thing that caught my eye was: Marriage Certificate, in bold black letters at the top. My eyes scanned each line on the document until I reached the bottom, where both my and his signatures were. I squinted and held the document closer to my face in shock.

"Constatin. All jokes aside, how did you get my signature on this, and what did you do with these documents?" My voice had lowered to almost a whisper. A throbbing pain was starting to form in the center of my forehead.

How in the hell did my signature get on these damn papers?!

"You signed your signature at the hospital today. I am unsure how Mr. Legend got you to sign the documents, but you did. The documents were then taken to the probate office, where I paid a couple thousand dollars to get them filed, and the official documents hastened. You are legally my wife, Ari, and you will be my wife until the day you die."

Memories of the conversation I had with my charge nurse earlier today started floating back to me. She had me sign some documents, but there was so much going on that I didn't even look at what I signed. Now that I think about it, she didn't mention what the papers were for—she just pointed to the lines and told me to sign them.

"We are getting a divorce, and I am suing the fuck out of that hospital!" I angrily replied.

"No, we will not, and no, you are not."

His voice had hardened when he spoke, and for the first time tonight, I feared for my life.

"You can have anybody you want. Why are you doing this? Even with the limp, you are a rich and handsome man. I don't understand any of this."

"My reasons do not concern you. What is done is done," he stoically decreed.

Fuck that shit.

"I will be filing for divorce from you tomorrow. None of this shit is okay. You are fucking insane for even going to such lengths to force a woman to marry your crazy ass!"

"I do not like repeating myself. We will not be getting a divorce. I am the Nasu of the Romanian Mafia, and you will not embarrass me!"

"MAFIA? OH, HELL NAW. I AM NOT ABOUT TO LOSE MY LIFE FOR A MARRIAGE I DON'T EVEN WANT!" I yelled.

Silence filled the room. Constatin stared at me, clearly upset, as if I was the one in the wrong.

If he is mafia, so is his brother. Kenya done lost her goddamn mind.

The sound of the kitchen chair scrapping had my heartbeat speeding up. Constatin stood up from the table and strolled over to me. He stopped right beside my chair and leaned down to look at me.

"Divorce is not an option. One female has already humiliated me. There will not be another one. You have two choices, Ari; you can stay married to me, or you can die. What will it be?"

"Just kill me. I don't even care," I said.

The words were barely out of my mouth before I felt like my hair was being torn from my scalp. My body hit the floor and then dragged. I tried punching Constatin in his legs, my head hurting so bad that it was hard to remember which leg was the injured one. A door opened, and a bright light blinded me.

"Constatin! Stop! Please let me go!" was the last thing I remembered saying before my face was dunked into a tub full of water.

Constatin

Divorce! How dare she insult me like that. Does she not know who I am?!

Ari's face went under the water, and I held it there. She struggled, but I was too strong for her to get loose. Mentally, I counted to ninety seconds. A little after sixty seconds, her body went lax, and her hands fell to her side. The longer a person is submerged under water, the greater the chance of death. An average person can be submerged under water for one to three minutes before losing consciousness and ten minutes before dying.

After ninety seconds, I pulled Ari's head out of the water. She was unconscious, and her lips were turning blue. Carefully, I laid her body down on the bathroom floor and began CPR. I laced my fingers together and placed them directly over her chest. I did not want to crush any ribs, but I pushed down far enough to pump her heart. After I did thirty heart compressions, I lifted her head back and gave her two breaths. Immediately after the two breaths, I went back into the heart compressions.

On the nineteenth compression, Ari began to froth at the mouth. Delicately, I turned her head to the side. Water came out, and she coughed a few times. I waited until I was sure that she had spit up all the water before scooping down to pick her up. My leg was screaming in pain, but I ignored it. Ari had all her rags and towels on a small rack next to the bathroom sink. I picked up a rag and wiped her face off before putting the rag into the dirty clothes hamper. She was still gasping for air when I carried her upstairs to her bedroom. With my right hand, I pulled the top cover back on her bed and laid her down.

"No. Stop," she whispered weakly when I removed her wet shirt and tossed it on the floor.

Her bedroom was dark, and I did not know where she put her dirty clothes in there. She sniffled and stared straight ahead, avoiding my gaze. I stood there silently watching her while she calmed down enough to stop gasping for air every fifteen or so seconds. Tears started to flow down her cheeks.

"I do not give second chances, Ari, but I will this once, only because you are my wife. I will be a good husband to you. You do not have to worry about me cheating, and financially, you will be well taken care of. My life is a dangerous one, and I am a busy man, but I will always communicate openly with you. We can have a good life together if you decide that this is what you want. What will it be, Ari? Marriage or death?

She stopped crying and looked up at me. We stared at each other for a few seconds before I saw her eyes give in.

"Marriage," she answered before turning away from me and pulling the cover over her whole body.

"Excellent choice. You will need to move in immediately. If you stop by the office in the morning, I will have security follow you to the house to show you where you live now. Please do not try to run from me. For some reason, I do not want to have to kill you. Sleep well, and do not forget that I am your lifeline now," I told her.

Ari did not respond, but I did not expect her to.

Emet and Mikey were parked down the street, waiting for my call. I walked out of her bedroom and pulled my cellphone out to let them know I was ready. Today was a long day, but the goals I set were all accomplished.

Ari

My alarm woke me up this morning. If yesterday had been a regular day, I would have unplugged it before I went to bed so I could sleep in on my day off. It wasn't every day that a girl ended her night being drowned by her unwanted ass husband. My cellphone rang from the kitchen, but I didn't move to get up yet. With the kind of luck I was having, it was probably my husband calling to make sure I was coming into his office this morning.

Don't let anybody play in your face. The moment you do, you lose your power to them.

My mother's voice was clear in my thoughts. I closed my eyes and then breathed deeply before exhaling. If Constatin wanted a nice, obedient wife, who jumped when he said so, he should have married somebody else. I had no problem submitting to a man who made me feel safe and secure. All Constatin did was make me want to commit bodily harm with a deadly weapon.

Get up, girl. You got business to handle.

I said a quick prayer before rolling over and getting out of my bed. The next forty-five minutes were spent taking my shower and getting dressed. Now, I stood in front of my mirror, giving myself a final look over.

The sangria wide-legged pants and basil green slim-fit t-shirt were a cute mixture between looking classy and comfortable. My face was covered in a natural beat of make-up, with matching sangria-colored lips. The last thing I had to do was twist my braids up into a bun on top of my head before turning away from the mirror and leaving my bedroom. I was going to raise hell, but at least I will look good while doing it.

When I made it to my kitchen, my cellphone was still lying on the kitchen table. Anxiety ran through my body as I picked it up to see who had called me earlier. My best friend's picture popped up after I used my thumbprint to unlock it.

I love my best friend, but if she were in front of me now, I would choke the shit out of her.

Now, I knew why Kenya's voice had been full of concern the last few times we talked. She knew the devil himself was after me and didn't give me any kind of real warning. I put my phone back inside my purse and walked across the kitchen.

Over the last week, I had been so busy that I hadn't had time to grocery shop. I opened my refrigerator and pulled the milk out. The date said that it had expired. After twisting the red top off and sniffing it, the pungent smell proved that the milk was indeed expired. I set the milk cartoon on my kitchen counter and went to get the last few items I needed.

By nine-thirty, I was inside my car, pulling out of my driveway, and heading to my husband's job. I did not know much about Bucur Wine International other than what Google told me when I searched for the address to put into my GPS.

The ride to Bucur Wine International was lit. My favorite playlist had me singing and rapping the whole way there. My throat was sore, giving my voice a slight raspiness, but that didn't stop me from singing and rapping like I was at a concert.

The parking lot of Bucur Wine International was not only packed, but I had to pay a thirty-dollar valet fee. My dear husband was going to hear my mouth about that as soon as I made it to his office. Bucur Wine International was in a building the size of a mall. When I walked inside, I had to walk through a metal detector that was guarded by two mean-mugging security guards.

Your husband is in the Mafia. Of course, security is going to be tight.

After passing security, I walked up to the woman at the desk who was handing other people passes. She was a Caucasian woman with brown eyes and long black hair that she had pulled back into a ponytail.

"Good morning. I am here to see Constantin," I informed her.

The lady frowned before looking me up and down.

"Mr. Bucur is seen by appointment only. He does not take walk-ins," she rudely replied.

"Ma'am, today is not the day. Call and tell him that his WIFE is here to see him. Please and thank you," I snapped.

Normally, I would have more patience, but I didn't even want to be there in the first place. The lady's eyes went to my left hand and locked onto my empty ring finger.

This lady is going to piss me off.

"Mrs. Bucur. Right this way," a male voice said from behind me.

The lady looked behind me in shock. I glanced over my shoulder and smiled when I saw one of Constatin's security guards. Without saying another word to the lady at the desk, I turned around and followed the security guard to the elevators. The elevator had soft classical music playing on it, and I hummed along to it. When we got off the elevator, the secretary gave me a big smile and a small wave.

Hmmm. Constatin must have told her about this sham of a marriage.

I returned the smile and followed the security guard to my husband's office. He didn't go inside the office. Instead, he opened the door and held it for me to walk through.

"Thank you," I mumbled as I passed him.

"What's up, Ari?" Kofi said to me when I walked inside.

"Hey," I replied politely, without glancing at him.

His sister was still on my shit list, and I wasn't ready to talk to her and her brother yet. My eyes quickly looked around my husband's office, not surprised at all by the way it looked. His office had no personality at all. Everything was either black or grey in color. There weren't any art or family pictures displayed on the wall, and it smelled like nothing but a faint scent of his cologne.

"Excuse me," Kofi said as he passed me on the way out of the office.

I stepped aside and waited for him to leave before glancing at my husband sitting at his desk.

"Come have a seat," Constatin stated.

"Do you have any manners at all? That is not how you greet people, especially the woman you are married to," I huffed out before walking over to have a seat at the chair in front of his desk.

"Actually, my mother did instill the importance of manners into me and my brothers. I just do not have a use for such frivolous words," he smartly replied.

I am going to end up on an episode of Snapped.

Instead of replying, I just shook my head in disgust. My mom always told me to be careful what I wished for. For years, I prayed to God and asked him to marry me to a rich man with a big dick, and now look at me: Stuck with the spawn of Lucifer.

I wonder if his package matches his wallet.

My eyes quickly moved to my husband's pants and then shifted before he could see what had caught my attention.

The bastard gives off big dick energy. I bet every dollar in my empty ass bank account that his mean ass is blessed.

"Until I have time to hire and vet you your own security detail, Mikey is going to stay with you everywhere you go. Unless you have a question of importance, refrain from conversing with him. He knows only to speak to you when necessary."

Constatin pulled out a drawer in his desk and handed me a set of two keys and a black credit card with his name on it.

"Mikey knows the security code. Once you have proven that you are trustworthy, I will give it to you."

"If I use the card, am I going to go to jail?" I asked.

"No, I added you to the account this morning. There is no limit on it. You can use it for all your needs."

"Hmmm," I replied and slid both the card and the keys into my purse. I was going to spend his money regardless, but if he thought giving me money could buy me, he was in for a rude awakening.

"Don't you have anything else you want to say to me?" I asked.

He looked at me, puzzled, clearly confused by my question.

"Ari, I have a meeting in twelve minutes. What is it that you want to know?" he asked impatiently.

"I want my husband to apologize for fucking drowning me."

"No. I will be home later. Mikey will show you which bedroom is ours. Too much clutter overstimulates me. I expect everything to be put away before I get home. If you need to go shopping, Mikey will take you," he replied, dismissing me.

Un-fucking-believable.

At that point, Ashton Kutcher could've jumped out at any moment and yelled, 'Punk'd!' because this can't be my life. It must be some kind of prank. Seconds passed before the harsh reality was crystal clear.

"Mr. Husband. It might be a good idea to get me a wedding ring. The bitch downstairs didn't want to let me up because my ring finger is empty," I told him as I stood up to leave.

His eyes narrowed at my use of vulgar language.

"Mrs. Wife. What part of 'The card in your purse does not have a limit' did you not understand?"

My response to that was slamming his office door on the way out. There I was, a grown ass twenty-two-year-old nurse, behaving like an infant. But I couldn't help it. The man got under my skin and triggered the hell out of me.

Mikey silently followed me on my way to the elevator. In the parking lot, he got inside my car as soon as I unlocked the door. The only words the man spoke on the ride to Constatin's house were to give me directions. Constatin stayed half an hour away from where he worked. The closer I got to his house, the more I felt my body perspiring. Every house I passed looked like it could belong to Jay-Z and Beyoncé.

"Pull up to the black iron gate right there," Mikey directed while pointing. My mouth dropped open when I pulled up in front of the home he pointed to. A guard walked to the gate, and Mikey let the window down to show his face.

Damn, how much security does one person need?

"Your house is Ancient Roman inspired and situated on two acres of land. It has approximately 8,590 square feet of living space. There are seven bedrooms, full bathrooms, a foyer with a staircase, a formal living and dining room, kitchen, rear staircase, rec room with a wet bar, a wine cellar that you are not allowed in, home theater, three car garage, gun range, and a pool house," Mikey ranted off as I pulled in.

"Did your boss really make you memorize all the details of his home?" I questioned.

"Yes, ma'am, he did this morning. He wanted you to know everything because he doesn't have time to give you a tour."

"Hmmmm."

I noticed a few more security guards scattered around the property as I drove up the mile-long driveway.

"Do all of the security guards stay on the premises?"

"Only Mikey and I stay in the residence. The other security guards rotate shifts. But there is always security on the premises," he informed me.

If I needed to escape, it wouldn't be easy to get away now that I am being forced to move in with him.

Once my car was parked in front of Constatin's home, I got out and hit the trunk button on my key fob. Mikey followed me to the trunk to get the one and only suitcase I brought. He stopped me before I could pull it out and grabbed it for me instead. I followed him to the front of the property, where he unlocked the door and then entered a code into the alarm after we walked in.

Constatin's home was beautiful. He had a big ass crystal chandelier that hung in the foyer as soon as you entered the home, and it screamed wealth.

"Right this way."

Mikey walked down the foyer toward the gold spiral staircase. We walked up the stairs and took a left. All the doors were open, and I saw that each bedroom and bathroom we passed was beautifully decorated. Constatin didn't strike me as the decorating type. I assumed he hired an interior decorator for his whole home.

If this were a real marriage, I would have preferred to decorate my own home.

"Constatin wants you to share bed chambers. His room is through this door right here," Mikey pointed to the only room with the door closed. He twisted the doorknob, and we walked inside.

The man had no personality at all. Everything in his room was bland. The bed was bigger than a California King size and had to have been custom-made.

"The closet is right through that door, and the bathroom is straight ahead. The kitchen is fully stocked, and you are allowed in every room in the house except the wine cellar."

It's probably dead bodies in the wine cellar. Imma end up in federal prison dealing with this bullshit.

Mikey handed me my suitcase and walked out, leaving me by myself. A couple of minutes passed by, and I was just taking in my surroundings before I laid my suitcase flat on the floor. I crouched down on the floor and unzipped it. For the first time all day, I smiled.

Inside my suitcase was my metal bat, a can of bear mace, and a spray bottle that I filled with rotten milk. Time was of the essence, and I knew I only had about forty-five minutes to fuck up as much shit as possible. The first thing I did was clip the bear mace onto my pants, take the spray bottle with milk, and spray it all over his bed and then the furniture in the room. Then, I walked into his closet and laughed hysterically.

By the time night came, he would have to replace everything I sprayed with rotten milk because it was going to smell atrocious the longer it sat. Quickly, I flipped through his clothes, spraying the rotten milk on everything. Five minutes later, I exited the closet and walked to his bedroom window.

The metal bat smashed both windows, causing glass to fly everywhere. Next, I busted out the glass window on his dresser. Not even a minute later, Mikey came running back into Constatin's bedroom, but he was expected.

"What the hell is going on?!" he yelled and then froze.

"You can't shoot me because Constatin will kill you for touching his wife, and if you get within six feet of me, I will bear mace the shit out of you," I warned him.

The bear mace was still clipped to my pants, but it had stretched out so I could hold it in my hand, pointed straight ahead, ready to spray him if he got any closer. Mikey threw his hands up and slowly backed out of the room.

My next stop was the living and dining room, but I smashed every picture in the hallway on the way there. Mikey was on the phone with Constatin by the time I made it down the stairs, but he stayed a safe distance away from me. In the living room and dining room, I sprayed all the furniture with rotten milk and then smashed every window and vase I could reach.

By the time I finished, I was exhausted, but pure rage had me moving to the kitchen to get myself a chair. Mikey stared at me like I was a mad woman when I pulled a kitchen chair from the table and dragged it to the foyer. I put the chair close enough under the chandelier so that when I swung my bat, I could hit it. But I left enough room for me to jump out of the way when it came crashing down. Tired, I took a few deep breaths while standing in the kitchen chair before I reached up and swung the bat as hard as I could.

"Fuck!" I whined when I hit the floor.

The chandelier came crashing down so fast that I almost jumped a second too late and killed my own damn self. My ankle was hurting when I stood back up, but I limped down the foyer in pain, smashing pictures along the way.

"If you swing that bat one more fucking time, I will kill your crazy ass!" my husband yelled from the front door.

Finally! My adrenaline was fading, and my whole body felt sore.

"Welcome home, husband!" I said with a smile on my face.

Constatin shot me a look full of hatred. He walked all the way into the house and snatched the bat out of my hand. I let it go and laughed.

"I have married a crazy catea (bitch)," he mumbled as he walked past me toward the stairs.

I hobbled back to the kitchen to have a seat and wait for my dear husband to assess the damages. Mikey shook his head but kept his ass far away from me while his boss was gone. Constatin came back down the stairs ten minutes later.

"Get up. Let's go," he demanded.

"No. If you are planning to kill me, do it here. I don't feel like moving."

"If I had not already announced our marriage, trust me, you would have been dead the second I walked through the door. Now, get up, Ari. It is a mess, and I do not like it." The last time his voice hardened like that, he dunked my head in a tub full of water.

I got up and hobbled over to him. My ankle felt like it was swelling. Jumping from a chair wasn't the smartest idea, but I would do it again in a heartbeat.

Constatin walked outside to his car, where Emet waited. Emet looked like he wanted to laugh, but he knew he would die if he did. That made me chuckle. My husband cut his eyes at me before opening the passenger side door on his grey Rolls Royce Phantom for me. Shocked, I mumbled thanks and got inside his car.

"Where are we going?" I asked him when he got in the car.

Constatin didn't answer me. He waited for Emet to pull out of the driveway and followed him. I glanced in the rear-view mirror and noticed Mikey was trailing in the black Mercedes Benz behind us. Exhausted, I laid my head back and closed my eyes.

"Get up." My husband roughly shook me.

Slowly, I opened my eyes and yawned. Constatin got out of his car and walked around to the passenger side door to open it. My ankle was hurting even more now. Gently, I slid out of his car and leaned against it while he shut the door. We were parked in front of a nice penthouse apartment complex.

"You have a penthouse here?" I asked him.

Instead of answering, he waited for his security guards to park before he turned away from me to walk to the valet.

"Good morning, Mr. Bucur," the valet greeted Constatin.

I guess that answers my question.

"Park all three vehicles in our normal spots," Constatin replied before reaching into his pants pockets and pulling out his wallet.

Constatin pulled a hundred-dollar bill out of his wallet and handed it to the valet. He then patted the guy on the shoulder and walked into the apartment complex. I limped behind him with Emet and Mikey following closely behind me.

There weren't a lot of people in the lobby of the apartment complex, but the few people who were there all stopped what they were doing to stare at us. If I saw two people with limps walking by, followed by security guards, I would stare, too.

"Good morning, Mr. Bucur," the woman standing at the desk spoke.

My rude ass husband didn't respond. He walked past her to the elevators.

Everybody here knew him by name. He must come here often. It's probably where he entertains his whores.

For some reason, that thought made me mad, and I frowned.

"Mrs. Bucur appears to be in a lot of pain. Would you like one of us to carry her for you?" Emet asked my husband as we entered the elevator.

"Touch my wife, and I will cut off your hand," Constatin replied nonchalantly. I glanced back at Emet, and his face had turned bright red.

"Stop being so mean. At least he cares about my injury," I retorted.

"If you had not been destroying property that did not belong to you, you would not be in pain. Nonetheless, I am the only person who will take care of you, and I will only do so when I see fit."

It was on the tip of my tongue to remind my husband that what was his was mine, but I underestimated how much energy it took to destroy a mansion. All I wanted to do was eat something and curl up in bed to watch one of my favorite shows.

The elevator went to the top floor and stopped.

I was surprised to see that there were only two penthouse apartments on the whole floor. There was one penthouse on the left side of the hallway and one right across on the right. Constatin walked to the penthouse on the right and used a swipe card to unlock the door. The penthouse was enormous inside, but I expected nothing less.

My husband was a wealthy man, but money didn't impress me. I wouldn't date a man who did not make more than me. But there were plenty of men who had money and who weren't psychopaths.

Emet and Mikey didn't follow us into the penthouse. They both stood outside the door, where I assumed they would stay. Constatin walked to the stairs, but I paused briefly to look at the floor-to-ceiling windows in the living room. From what I could see, the view of downtown Atlanta was amazing.

"Ari," my husband called my name impatiently.

Every step I climbed behind him had a sharp pain shooting from my ankle and up my leg. My ankle wasn't broken because I was able to put pressure on it and walk, but it needed to be iced and elevated.

Upstairs, there was only one bedroom. Constatin opened the bedroom door and held it for me to wobble inside. I wobbled all the way to the edge of his bed and sat down. Constatin disappeared into the bathroom. When he came back out, he had a black bag in his hand.

"The suitcase you brought was laid empty on the bedroom floor at the house. You will have to find something of mine to wear until we have time to get your belongings. You will not be going anywhere else today. Use the card I gave you to order some food and whatever else you want. Mikey will stay here with you. The front desk clerk will alert Mikey when your food or packages arrive, and he will get them. The only people who have access to the floor are me and my security." Constatin sat beside me on the bed as he talked.

"It must be nice to afford to rent a penthouse to stay in whenever you see fit," I mumbled.

"I am the owner of the whole complex. Well, technically, we both do. Hand me your left foot." His voice left no room for argument.

Confused, I turned to the side and lifted my left foot. He reached down to pick my foot up and placed it in his lap.

"Ouch," I whined, but he ignored me. Constatin opened the black bag and took out some kind of spray and elastic bandage.

"This antiseptic solution will clean the area," he informed me before rolling my pants leg up.

He sprayed my ankle with the solution and then used the elastic bandage to wrap my ankle. Surprisingly, he was gentle in his movements, shocking me. After wrapping my ankle, he stood and walked to the head of the bed to pick up a pillow. He used that pillow to elevate my ankle, causing the pain I was feeling to decrease immensely. Constatin put the items back in the bag and took them back to his bathroom.

"You have caused me to waste time that I did not have to

waste. I am going back to work. It will be late when I return. Do not wait up for me," my husband stated when he came out of the bathroom.

He continued walking from the bathroom out of the bedroom. I thought he had left the penthouse when he returned a few minutes later with ice cubes inside a Ziploc bag.

"Here." He handed the ice bag to me.

"Thank you," I softly replied.

Constatin's actions surprised me. From what he had shown me of his character, I did not think he cared about anybody but himself. It was on the tip of my tongue to ask him about the stitches I put in his arm, but I doubted he would tell me, so I kept my thoughts to myself.

"You should be able to order a ring and have it delivered."

I laughed before responding to his statement. "Of course, I can, but I won't. What I look like purchasing my own wedding ring? If you want me to wear one, I suggest you make time in your busy ass schedule to purchase one."

Constatin huffed, clearly aggravated by my response.

He walked over to the nightstand to pick up the TV remote. Constatin handed the remote to me and walked back out of the bedroom. This time, he did not return.

Constatin

It had been a few hours since I returned to work, and I had been receiving messages from Mikey, keeping me updated on my wife. He did not have to tell me that she had changed into one of my Moncler t-shirts and a pair of my briefs before climbing into bed, where she had remained.

My penthouse had cameras in every room, including the bathroom, and I had been checking them periodically. He informed me that she had ordered some takeout food from Mellow Mushroom and hygiene products and clothes from Target. I had approved the items after he checked them in the lobby.

Mikey was instructed to enter the penthouse and take them to her. He knocked and waited for her to answer before entering the bedroom so he would not scare her. Mikey placed her items on the bed and rushed back out of the bedroom and then out the front door. I watched the cameras closely to make sure he followed directions. If he had muttered one word to her, he would have lost his tongue when I returned tonight.

A knock at the door had me turning my head away from my computer screen to glance up. I knew it was Kofi because he was the only person who knocked. My brothers just barged in, and my secretary called my office phone every time before approaching my office door. Kofi waited a few seconds before walking into my office with his laptop in his hand.

"I know where the police chief and his wife are."

Kofi had walked up to my desk but did not have a seat.

"Where are they?" I asked.

"A cabin an hour and a half away in Cleveland, Georgia. His wife has a shopping addiction, and she loves shoes. She frequently buys from Saint Laurent. I sent an ad to her email address that appeared to be from them about a sale on some high heels that she had pinned to her Pinterest board. She clicked the link, and it pinged her location and sent it to me. The cabin is in the name of a police officer who works in the same precinct. It was a smart idea because the officer wasn't related to him or in his close friend group."

"How many cabins are close by?"

"A total of eight, but they are spread out in the woods to ensure the customers' privacy," Kofi answered.

Good. Fear causes people to make irrational decisions. His death was high on the extensive list of things I needed to carry out that I would be glad to cross off.

Normally, I would go alert my brothers that we had a mission to do tonight. But, after peering at Kofi, I decided tonight would be a perfect opportunity to kill two birds with one stone. As the Nasu, there really was not a need for me to get my hands dirty, but this was a personal matter that should have been handled a couple of months ago.

"Are you positive that being a Capo is what you want?" I asked Kofi. His face changed, no longer appearing friendly, and I could sense the excitement coursing through his body.

"I am positive," he confirmed.

"Tonight, we will go hunting. Just me, you, and Emet. Wait until the building is empty and come back to my office," I replied before turning back to the computer to continue what I was doing before he entered. Kofi was familial (family) to me. But, if he failed tonight, I would reconsider involving him any deeper.

"Yes, sir," he replied, nodding his head.

Kofi left my office, and I leaned back in my desk chair. My marriage was already costing me millions. The cleaning crew I had to hire to clean up my mansion that she destroyed said that it could take a few days before I would be able to come by and see what I needed to have replaced. Our marriage would work, though. Failing again was not an option.

The rest of my day was spent catching up on the work I missed. Bucur Wine International was on the verge of doing an exclusivity deal with Bellagio. Bellagio was willing to pay eight figures to be the only hotel in the world to carry a new white and red wine that we had been perfecting for the last four years. The chairperson of the Board of Directors for Bellagio was scheduled to fly in tomorrow with his lawyers to finalize the deal. This would be our third time meeting in the last six months, and I was confident that the deal would go through as planned.

As the new chairperson of the board of directors for Bucur Wine International, my mind was bursting with new venture ideas that I had been working on in preparation for this moment. In hindsight, I was under the impression that I would not take over the Board from my father for at least ten more years.

Sadly, I underestimated life's ability to make a mockery of the plans I had. Thinking of my father had me pulling out the bottom drawer on my desk and taking out the bottle of Highland Park and a glass cup. Quickly, I fixed myself a double shot of the liquor and drank it.

The temptation to continue taking shots until I no longer felt the pain from my father's death and the circumstances surrounding it was strong. But I fought the temptation and placed the items back into my bottom desk drawer. Becoming an alcoholic would be a disgrace to my father and all the years he spent preparing me to take over as the Nasu of the mafia and run Bucur Wine International.

The liquor coursed through my body, calming my nerves, but I still felt antsy. I picked my cell phone up from my desk and went into the camera app to check on my wife. All day, I had found myself pausing in the middle of work to check on Ari. Perhaps it was because of the way she behaved earlier.

Before I could ponder the reasons more, there was a knock on my door. The time on my phone read seven-seventeen at night, and I knew the workers and security had all vacated the premises. Kofi entered my office a few moments later and stood by the door, waiting for me. It only took me a few minutes to shut everything down and slide my suit jacket back on. Kofi, Emet, and I left the company's parking lot ten minutes later.

Emet had already been informed of my plans and knew where we were going. On the ride to Cleveland, Georgia, Kofi and I spent the time knocking out simple tasks that could be done from our phones. It was almost ten at night when Emet took a turn into the woods where the cabins in Cleveland were. The woods were vast and went on for miles and miles. Emet drove for ten more minutes before pulling to the side and parking.

"The cabin is four minutes ahead," he announced.

I slid my phone into my pocket and pulled my Beretta M9A3 from my waistband. The plan was to be in and out, so I attached my suppressor to the end of it.

"Do I need to put my suppressor on my Smith and Wesson?" Kofi asked, and I nodded. Kofi attached his suppressor to his gun before we exited the car.

All three of us walked as silently as we could through the woods to where the cabin was located. The cabin had two lights on inside it when we approached. I signaled for Emet to do a quick perimeter check. Emet and Mikey were ex-military. They both used to work for Tom before he betrayed us and ran. Emet did the perimeter check and pointed toward a window. We all crept to the window to see the police chief and his wife sitting at the kitchen table, eating.

I pointed to the back of the cabin, letting Emet know that we would break in the back door and catch them by surprise. Emet nodded, and we followed him to the back door of the cabin. My father always told me that there were two kinds of police officers. There were the police officers who had a natural ability to put several different pieces together to solve a crime, and then you had the police officers with a lower level of intelligence. Those police officers liked to use force and scare tactics to solve crimes. The police chief was the latter. Emet broke into the back door of the cabin in under a minute.

We quietly walked through the living room to the kitchen. There was only one entrance to the kitchen. We had to move swiftly to silence them. I pointed to the police chief's wife, who had her back turned to us, and rushed into the kitchen. The police chief heard us coming, but my gun was pressed into the side of his wife's head before he could move.

"If you scream, I will kill her," I warned him.

His wife shrieked, but after I pushed the nozzle of my gun harder into the side of her head, she shut up.

"Please don't kill us. Let me explain. Officer Mill had run his mouth to a few other officers in the precinct. Officers who weren't on your payroll. He told them if anything happened to them, that Alexandur did it. Now, I was not informed of this until after their dead bodies were tossed on my lawn. If I didn't send the officers to question Alexandur, it would have been suspicious," the police chief begged me.

His wife was now crying and sniffling, but it was not loud. I lowered my gun and smiled at the police chief.

"Why did you not come to us?" I asked him, taking a seat at the kitchen table.

Relief flooded his face, and he placed a hand over his heart.

"You guys aren't the most understanding. I needed time to figure out what to do next, and I had vacation time saved. I figured in a couple of weeks, you guys would have calmed down enough for me to approach one of you and explain."

He sounded sincere, and I knew he was telling the truth. I gave Kofi a slight head nod. He lifted his gun and shot the police chief's wife through the side of her head. Her head fell onto the kitchen table with blood pouring out the side of it. The police chief gasped and looked at me in shock. I let off all seventeen rounds in my gun into his face and chest. Without touching anything, I stood, and we left back the same way we came in.

The only reason the police chief and his wife's bodies would be found eventually was to send a warning to the police officers at the precinct that the mafia was not to be fucked with. Kofi was the only one with a few blood splatters on him. In the car, on the way back to Atlanta, I made him take his shirt off and hand it to me. He did so, silently staring off into space for the rest of the ride home. When we made it back to Atlanta, I properly disposed of his shirt before Emet dropped him back off at his vehicle.

He had done good for his first kill. He did not hesitate and held his aim steady like I taught him. Mentally, the kill would bother him until he killed a few more times. Then, it would become second nature.

Ari was asleep by the time I entered the penthouse, as I expected. I showered and climbed into bed with her. My body was turned away from her and facing the bedroom door. It did not take long for me to drift off to sleep.

ARI

The last two days were spent doing exactly what I wanted. Today, I was scheduled to return to work, and I felt motivated and refreshed. The swelling in my ankle had gone down, and I was back moving around freely.

My husband and I hadn't said anything to each other. I hadn't even seen him. If it weren't for the scent of his Baccarat cologne still lingering in the room and the sheets being rumpled on his side of the bed, I would have thought he had not returned to the penthouse at all. When I destroyed his bedroom at the mansion, I made sure to crash his Baccarat cologne bottle. Imagine my surprise when one of the first items I saw on his dresser here was another bottle of Baccarat.

After a quick stretch, I climbed out of bed. Before going to take my shower, I made the bed up. In the closet was a new pair of scrubs that I had purchased and gotten delivered yesterday. Eventually, I would go to the house and get some of my belongings, but I was not in a rush. I used his black card to buy anything I needed. There was no point in bringing all the stuff there anyway, just to have to move it all again.

After I showered, I did the rest of my hygiene routine and got dressed. I applied some lip gloss and left the bedroom. Before going to work, I planned to make myself a cup of coffee but forgot all about it when I entered the kitchen.

"What are you doing here?"

Constatin was sitting at the marble island, scaring the hell out of me.

"Thanks to you, I live here now. The cleaners called me this morning, fussing about the whole house smelling rotten and them being unable to get the scent out of my furniture."

"I bet next time you will think twice before attempting to kill me," I replied and then laughed.

"If I wanted you dead, you would be. I do not do attempts."

"Whatever. Is that why you're here?"

"No, actually, it is to inform you that you no longer work at the hospital."

What the fuck did he just say?

"What do you mean?" I asked him, confused.

Did I get fired from the hospital and didn't know about it?

"I called Mr. Legend this morning and informed him of your resignation," he stated.

I would have done anything to have a gun in my hand at that moment.

"Constatin, why the fuck would you do that? I am going to work today!" I screamed at the top of my lungs to the crazy ass man.

"No, you are not. The hospital is impossible to secure for an extended amount of time. There are too many entrances and people who could get close enough to cause you harm. It is my job, as your husband, to keep you safe."

For a minute, I just stared at him. My life wouldn't even be in danger if it wasn't for him.

"I like my job. I worked hard to become a nurse and help people. Now, you are telling me that I can't work in my field because my husband is a fucking criminal when I didn't even want his criminal ass to be my husband in the first place!"

"Precisely. Maybe in the future, you can own your own practice or do medical work online. But working at a major hospital will not be acceptable."

Tears dropped down my face, and I angrily wiped them away. My whole body was shaking in anger, and he just sat there calmly.

"I hate you."

"Hating me is fine. It will not change the facts, though. If you disobey me and step one foot into that hospital, I will bomb it. The blood of the people who are killed will be on your hands."

Oh, my God! What did I do to deserve such a cruel ass man?

"So, what am I supposed to do all day? Sit here like a fucking puppy and wait for you to come home?"

"There you go, being dramatic again. This afternoon, Mikey will be taking you to meet with Kenya to go dress shopping and get a tattoo. The familial (families) are throwing us a gala to officially welcome me as the Nasu and you as my wife. You will be acting as regina mea (my queen) during the gala, and you will not embarrass me."

"Fuck you. Fuck that gala, and fuck all that Romanian bullshit you just said, too," I replied before turning away and going back up the stairs.

As soon as I opened the bedroom door, I locked it and slid to the floor to cry. I sat on the bedroom floor and cried until I had no more tears left in me. My cellphone dinged and alerted me of a text message. My mother had called a few times over the last few days, but I hadn't answered. She and I were like best friends, and I was scared that if she heard my voice, she would know something was wrong.

Get up and text her back. If you don't, she will be on the first plane out here, and then all hell is really going to break loose.

My insides were full of sorrow as I stood and walked over to the nightstand, where my phone was. After unlocking the screen, a text message from an unknown number popped up.

Unknown: When you stop crying, go downstairs to eat some breakfast and drink some water to hydrate. Mikey will be waiting for you in exactly two hours to take you to meet Kenya.

How did he know I was crying?

My head moved left to right, looking around the room before a crazy answer popped into my head.

Me: Do you have cameras in here?

Unknown: Stop frowning and yes

I dropped my phone onto the carpet and screamed in frustration. Constatin's ass needed to be at the top of the FBI's Most Wanted List, not running a multi-billion dollar international wine corporation.

Nonetheless, two hours later, I walked out of the bedroom and down the stairs. I still had on the pink scrubs and matching pink closed-toed crocs I put on to go to work this morning. If today was going to be the last day I wore scrubs for a while, I was going to wear them all day long. On the way to the front door, a black ring box on the kitchen island caught my eye.

Did he buy me a wedding ring like I asked?

I turned around and went to the kitchen to pick up the black ring box. For some reason, my right hand shook a little when I flipped open the ring box. A smirk appeared on my face, and I rolled my eyes. The ring staring back at me was perfect. It was a simple oval diamond ring on a gold band. The diamond sparkled as I lifted the ring out of the box, and the cursive letters engraved on the inside of the gold band caught my eye. I brought the ring up closer to my eyes to see what it said. "Regina mea," I said aloud. Constatin had said the same words earlier when he was talking about going to that gala.

"Siri. What does 'regina mea' mean in Romanian?" I asked my phone while sliding the ring onto my ring finger. It fit perfectly, but I wasn't surprised, considering my husband was a stalker who liked to invade my privacy.

The Romanian term 'regina mea' is translated as 'my queen' in English," Siri replied.

Constatin wanting me to act like his queen at the gala, while he had done nothing but act like a devil to me, was mind-boggling. The front door of the penthouse opened, and Mikey stuck his head inside.

"Mrs. Bucur, your husband just called. We are late leaving and must go now."

"Coming!" I replied before walking out of the kitchen and then out the front door.

Mikey led me down to the lobby and out to the parking lot. The valet already had the car pulled around when we walked out. Mikey opened the back door for me, and I climbed inside the car. A few minutes later, we were off to meet with Kenya.

Fifteen minutes later, Mikey pulled up to a boutique called Susan Lee.

"Mrs. Bucur is already inside. The store has been cleared out for the next two hours," Mikey informed me after opening the door so I could get out.

"Thank you," I replied, and he gave me a head nod.

Kenya jumped up and rushed toward me as soon as I walked through the boutique doors. I put my hand out to stop her from jumping into my arms.

"Are you mad at me?" she asked, laughing.

"Girl, if you weren't my best friend, I could murder you with my bare hands."

"If I had known Constatin was going to choose you at my wedding, I would have told you. His decision caught everyone off guard, including his brothers."

My eyes scanned my best friend. She was glowing and genuinely appeared to be happy.

"How come you got the good brother, and I got the psychopath?" I asked her, pouting.

"Come on. Let's talk while we look through dresses."

We walked toward a rack of dresses on the left, and I waited for her to answer.

"My husband is not a good man, Ari. In fact, he is known as the monster. I accept him as he is. He is more than I could ever dream of, and I love him with every inch of my heart," Kenya said.

My best friend has clearly gone off the deep end, but imma stand beside her.

"Hmmm, well, lucky you. Constatin is mean as hell. He tricked me into marrying him, and the only way out of this marriage is death," I whispered. The store clerks were close enough that we could call them for help if we needed to, but not close enough to come off as rude.

"Ari, I know you. Alexandur told me what you did to his mansion. He might be mean, but you know how to dish that shit right back at him."

Of course, she was right. But who wanted to be stuck in a marriage with their enemy for the rest of their life.

"You suck at being my best friend. You were supposed to tell me that he isn't as bad as he seemed," I whined.

"Before, when I found out he was pursing you, I couldn't say much. Now that y'all are married, I can speak more freely. Constatin is known as *The Mind*. From the time he was born, he was raised to be the Nasu of the Mafia and to run the family business. Constatin's father was getting ready to hand the reigns to Constatin when I met them. In order for Constatin to become the Nasu, he had to marry and produce an heir within a year of that marriage."

"An heir? As in a child? As in, he expects me to get pregnant and have a baby by his crazy ass?"

Constatin had only mentioned something about a baby once, and that was at the wedding. He was out of his mind if he thought he was sticking that demon dick inside me.

"Yes, it's not optional. The mafia is run just like a corporation. They have a board of directors from the most powerful mafia families, who oversee everyone to keep things in balance," she told me.

"Why are you talking about this as if it's normal? This shit is crazy!"

Kenya gave me a look of sympathy. It was clear she had accepted her fate, but this was a lot to take in.

"Ari, not only is it crazy, but it is serious. A couple of months ago, Constatin was betrayed by his fiancée and their head of security. He wasn't in love with his fiancée, but she had been his best friend for over twenty years. The bitch was planning to marry him and kill his whole family. She is the one who killed his father and shot him in the knee. She and Tom, the head of security, ran and have been in hiding since. Of course, the news travels fast. Be patient with him. He has a lot of pressure on him right now, and all the other mafia families are watching him closely. There had to be something about you that made him choose you as his bride. Yes, he was running out of time, but he could have anybody he wanted. I believe he will be an amazing husband, just like his brother."

What happened to him was terrible, but I wasn't convinced that he would become a good husband. My best friend was so happy, though, and I wasn't about to ruin that for her with my situation, so I changed the subject.

"Why am I getting a tattoo when we leave here?" I asked her.

"All members of the Romanian Mafia have a gold eagle tattooed on them. Everybody in the criminal world knows what that tattoo means, which is why you have to get it."

"Hmmmm," I replied.

Over the next hour, we shopped for the gala and got a couple of extra dresses for any future events. By the time we made it to the tattoo shop, Kenya and I were playing around and having fun. Being around her lifted my mood, and I felt a semblance of normalcy again.

She decided that we should get our tattoos in the same spot, and I agreed. I already had two other tattoos and was accustomed to the pain that came with getting them. Right before the man started my tattoo, I decided to add a queen crown on the head of the eagle.

Sadness came crashing back to me once the tattoo was finished, and it was time to part ways with Kenya. She promised we would hang together again soon, and I pretended to believe her. On the ride back to my prison cell, I silently cried again. My life had changed so much in a week, and I didn't know if I could survive it. I hadn't felt this helpless since the day I watched my daddy kill his brother.

Constatin

My wife had been even more distant after her outing with Kenya the other day. Contrary to what Ari believed, I took my duty as a husband seriously. The exclusive deal with Bellagio took a few more days than I expected, but my lawyer called me earlier to confirm it was now complete.

This was why I walked out of the office at five to go to the penthouse and spend time with her. My mother had called me earlier, upset because I had not brought Ari by to see her. Tomorrow was Saturday, and I was off. I promised I would bring Ari to have breakfast with her in the morning, and she calmed down. When I made it to the penthouse, Ari was upstairs lying in bed, holding her stomach.

"What is wrong with you?" I asked her.

"My menstruation came on yesterday, and my period cramps are killing me," she answered weakly.

"What can I do to make it better?"

"Jump off of a cliff," she drily replied.

I laughed, the sound almost foreign to my ears. Ari would not be Ari if she were not being difficult. Without saying another word, I walked out of the bedroom and went downstairs to have a seat on the recliner in the living room.

This was my first time living with a woman, and I only had basic knowledge about women and menstruation cycles. Instead of spending the next hour researching to learn all I could, I decided to call my mother back and ask her what to do.

"Fiul (son)," my mother said when she answered.

"My wife is experiencing cramps from her menstruation. How do I make them go away?"

My mother laughed before replying.

"Cramps are not easy to get rid of. The best thing for you to do is to order her some Midol, junk food, and a heating pad to soothe the cramps."

"I want them gone, Mother. Tell me how," I persisted.

"You are demanding, just like your father. Whenever my cramps became unbearable and medicine was not working, your father would make me cum. The next day, I would wake up painless."

A grimace crossed my face, and I hung up the phone. Over the next five minutes, I ordered the stuff to make my wife feel better. Twenty minutes later, I walked back up the stairs with a bunch of bags in my hands and some hot tea with honey.

Ari was still lying in the same position, but she had closed her eyes. I knew she was not sleep, though, because she was not snoring.

"Here"

Ari opened her eyes to look at me and moaned. She reached out to grab the tea and took a sip.

"This tea is good. What's in it?" she asked, sitting all the way up in the bed to drink more.

"Mostly peppermint and honey. It is similar to the tea my mother used to make for us when we were ill."

Ari nodded, and I watched as she drank the majority of the tea before placing the mug on the nightstand. She reached out to take the bags from me, and I handed them to her.

"Constatin, why is there so much candy and chocolate?" she asked, laughing.

"Reddit said that most women's favorite candy and period candy were different. I know your favorite candy is Skittles, but I ordered a bunch of chocolate and other candy, too."

"Oh, my God! Is that a heating pad? Ugh. I hate you, but you are heaven-sent right now."

Unsure how to respond, I remained quiet. Ari went through

the bag and pulled out a few chocolate bars before handing the bags back to me.

"Can you set them on the dresser? I will eat them all over the next few days."

I nodded and did as she asked. When I came back to bed, Ari plugged the heating pad up and put it on her stomach.

"Does the heating pad get rid of the cramps?" I questioned.

"No. Nothing does."

"I am about to go shower. When I get out, would you like to watch something on the television together?" I asked.

She looked at me in shock before slowly nodding her head. In the shower, I took my time washing my body. Thoughts of Ari's naked body every time she got naked to shower or get dressed had invaded my thoughts, causing my dick to get hard.

Calm down. Tonight is not about you.

Mentally, I tried to get my dick to soften, but he would not comply. I ended up jacking off before I got out. With only a towel wrapped around my waist, I exited the bathroom.

Ari had dropped the chocolate candy bar on top of her chest and was stretched out, snoring. I strolled to the bed and picked the candy bar up to throw it away when I spotted some melted chocolate right beside her bottom lip. I reached out to wipe some of it up with my thumb and then stuck my thumb in my mouth to taste the sweet morsel. After sucking my thumb dry, I walked away to toss the candy bar into the trash.

This time, when I returned to the bed, I reached down to unplug the heating pad and then pulled the coverlet off Ari. Ari always went to sleep in various kinds of long gowns that were three sizes too big for her. Her body was beautiful and only deserved to be clothed in the finest silk the world had to offer. I climbed into bed and spread her legs wide. The light in the bedroom was on, and I could see the outline of her pussy through the black cotton panties she had on. I removed her panties and tossed them to the floor.

"Ari," I called her name out, but she did not answer.

I only put one crushed Ambien in her tea because I did not want her to oversleep in the morning. My mother would be disappointed in me if we missed breakfast.

Slowly, I spread her legs, and my eyes feasted upon the prettiest set of pussy lips I had ever seen. Ari's pussy lips were thick, begging for me to touch them. My dick jumped under my towel, but I ignored him.

My right hand went to the white string that was hanging from her pussy, and I gently pulled the tampon out of her. Anticipation had me jumping off the bed and rushing to the toilet to flush the tampon and then climbing back onto the bed and between her legs. I inhaled the metallic scent of blood mixed with the earthy scent of her pussy before lifting her hips to taste her pussy. My tongue licked inside both of her pussy lips, acquainting the taste of her pussy to my taste buds before I slid my tongue inside.

Ari made a noise that almost made me devour her like a wild animal in the forest devoured its prey. But instead, I slid my tongue in and out of her pussy. The more I slid my tongue inside her, the more her blood coated it.

"Ummmmm," Ari moaned, still not fully awake.

My tongue slid from out of her pussy and up to her clit. Up and down, I licked her clit, until she was squirming in her sleep. It wasn't until my mouth closed around her clit, and I began to suck on it that she became aware of what was happening.

"Constatin?" she asked, her voice slurred from the Ambien.

"Yes, *regina* mea (my queen)," I stopped sucking her clit to answer.

The fact that she knew it was me, even in an altered state, had me sucking her clit back into my mouth with more pressure, determined to make her cum in my mouth. My wishes were granted a couple of minutes later when her legs began to tremble.

"Fill my mouth with your cum and blood, Ari," I demanded and bit down gently on her clit.

"AAGHHHHHHH!" Ari screamed, granting me my wish.

Like the animal I was, I sucked her pussy until there was no more cum or blood coming out of her. My dick had never been so hard in all my life, and I had been taught how to please a woman at the age of fifteen.

My father told me and my brothers that pussy was one of the most dangerous weapons in the world, and the only way to control it was to pleasure it to submission. For my fifteenth birthday, my father hired a professional woman to teach me everything about a woman's body, so I would not fall victim to the sinful pleasure good pussy could provide. My father told me that the day I came across some pussy that caused me to lose focus, I had to either marry the woman or kill her.

I got off the bed and went to the bathroom to get the wash that I watched Ari apply to her pussy every time she bathed and a wet rag. Like a good husband, I washed my wife's pussy and then tossed the rag into the dirty clothes hamper before taking another rag to wipe her pussy again to make sure that there was not any wash still left on her.

After tossing that rag in the hamper, I went to the rack where she kept her hygienic items and read the back of the blue and white tampon box. The instructions were simple. I unwrapped the tampon and went back to the bed to insert a new tampon inside my wife's pussy.

My dick was determined to be disobedient and remained hard the whole time. Determined not to give in, I walked away from Ari's side of the bed and climbed into the bed on my side.

"Come on," I spoke softly and then lifted Ari's body so that she could lie on me with her head on my chest.

Something told me that if Ari woke up in the puddle that her pussy, cum, and blood created, she would be upset, and tonight was all about ridding her body of pain.

Ari

"It's time to wake up," a male voice whispered into my ear.

I raised my hand to swat the noise and heard a smack. Confused, I slowly opened my eyes to see that I was lying on top of a man's chest. My memory was fuzzy, and I felt a little disoriented.

"We are having breakfast with my mother this morning. She is very eager and can't wait to officially meet you as my wife," Constatin said.

The natural woodsy smell of his body, mixed with the customized Baccarat cologne that he loved to wear, had me digging my face deeper into his chest to inhale. When I realized what I was doing, I tried to jump up, but Constatin had his arms wrapped around my body.

What the hell happened last night, and why is my mean ass husband holding me?

Frowning, I closed my eyes back to try to remember how I ended up in this position. The last thing I recalled was eating a chocolate bar and flipping through the channels to find a movie for us to watch. Constatin was being unusually nice to me. He even purchased me a heating pad that I'd had on my stomach. My eyes opened again, and I moved to sit up. This time, Constatin let my body go. My gaze flew to the side of the bed in search of the heating pad. It wasn't until I pulled the top cover back and spotted a wet spot with blood that flashes of something dark and sinful entered my mind.

No way. I have to be remembering some kind of weird, kinky dream.

The longer I stared at the wet spot, the more memories came back to me. Memories of me waking up to the feeling of ecstasy that I had never felt before. My eyes were heavy, and I remember calling my husband's name while trying to open them. A warm feeling began to build in my stomach, terrifying the shit out of me.

Why does the memory feel so real? Why am I turned on by something so disgusting?

"You are thinking so hard that it is causing wrinkles on the top of your head. Is there something you want to ask me?"

My head turned away from the wet spot to look the devil I married in his eyes.

"For some odd reason, I had a dream of you tasting my pussy while I was asleep. That's weird as fuck, right?"

Constantin smirked instead of answering. He looked amused, and something about that didn't sit right with me.

"My cycle is on. There is no way you would touch me down there, let alone lick me there, right? Especially while I was asleep. It had to be some kind of weird nightmare."

"Ari, a nightmare is when you have a frightening or unsettling dream. Neither of those two words describe how I made you feel last night. In fact, your body was feeling so much pleasure that you filled my mouth to the brim with your pussy, cum, and blood. It was quite delicious. If I were not in a rush to get you pregnant, I would love nothing more than to enjoy you on my tongue every month that you bleed."

My mouth flew open, and I stared at Constatin in disbelief.

"Are you saying you ate my pussy last night, knowing that I am on my menstruation cycle?"

"Ari, I did not just eat your pussy. I devoured you like a small child would a hot meal after being starved for days."

Who the fuck says some shit like that?

"Clearly, this has to be some kind of misunderstanding. It sounds like you are admitting to eating my bloody pussy while I was sleeping, and I know you would not do something like that."

Constatin has to be joking. There is just no way.

"If the simplistic term 'eating' is the term you choose to use to describe the way I feasted on the sweet treat between your legs, then yes, I did."

"What the fuck is wrong with you? Who lies like that? I would have never let you get that close to my pussy with your demonic ass tongue, asleep or not!"

"Precisely, which is why I drugged your tea."

I jumped out of bed so fast that I fell on the floor. This man was beyond insane. There wasn't a single word in the dictionary to describe the creature lying in bed in front of me.

"We really must get going. Disappointing my mother is a personal aversion of mine," he said.

"In what world would you think that I would want to spend time with you or your mother after admitting some psychotic shit like that? What reason would I have to want to be anywhere near you?"

God, not only am I married to a devil, but he is a vampire devil at that. You just be up there creating anything now, huh?

"My intentions were pure, *regina mea (*my queen). Yes, I enjoyed pleasing you, but my pleasure was not the motive. It is my duty as your husband to take your pain away, and after phoning my mother, I was informed that that was how my father eradicated my mother's cramps. Be honest, Ari. Have you experienced any cramps this morning?"

Well, I'll be damned. Let me sit back down.

Seconds passed while the truth swirled around in my brain. Constatin stared down at me, patiently waiting for my response.

"No, Constatin, I have not. But that does not excuse your actions."

"Wanting my actions excused would imply that I feel guilt for my behavior, and that is imprecise. We have wasted half an hour when this conversation could have been had in half that time. *Regina mea*, my only plan for today is to spend quality time with you. Can we put our differences aside for one day and enjoy each other's presence? Please do not deny me such a simple request. Give me a chance to show you that I can be a good husband to you."

This was the most time my husband had spent talking to me, and he sounded genuine. Mentally, I knew I shouldn't condone his actions. But another part of me wanted to cling to any hope that he and I could make our marriage work, even if it was false hope.

"My feelings are valid, and I am allowed to be upset by your actions. What you did was wrong, Constatin. But I am choosing to forgive you for the sake of this marriage. I do not want to spend the rest of my life married and miserable.

Constatin sat up in the bed, and I could see his dick print, hard and pushing against the towel he had around his waist. Until that very moment, I was not aware that he was damn near naked. My husband stood up, in all his fine ass glory, and reached his hand out to me. My hand joined his, and he helped me to my feet before leaning down to press a kiss onto my forehead.

There was a shift happening in the air surrounding us. It felt like we were being pulled together and thrown into a deep abyss, with only each other to cling to. If one of us failed the other, we would both drown and this time, there would be no coming back to life.

Constatin

My marriage was not a marriage of love, but I was beginning to feel a warmth toward my beautiful wife. I watched her closely from the corner of my eye. We had just pulled into my parents' driveway, and she had a look of amazement on her face.

"I thought your mansion was big, but it is nothing compared to this. Your parents' home is big enough to be converted into a high school or college."

"After the gala, we have to find a new home to move into. Whatever requirements and adornments you would like, just tell me, and I will make sure our new home is to your liking."

Ari was still gawking at my parent's home and only nodded her head in response.

The cleaning crew I hired was some of the best in the business, and after days of trying to scrub the foul scent out of my furniture and clothes, they called and informed me that nothing they did was working. I paid them extra for the effort and thanked them for their work. Now, I was having the whole house cleaned out. I instructed the contractors to donate what could be salvaged, but I wanted everything, including appliances, thrown away.

Eventually, I would get around to remodeling it. If my wife wanted us to keep it, we would. But, if not, it will be listed for sale.

Emet got out of the car and walked around to open my door for me. When I got out, I walked around and opened the door for Ari. I held my hand out to help her and then joined our hands together as we approached the front door. Mikey was already out of his vehicle and waiting for us to walk by him so he could trail us.

My brothers and I used to visit without our personal security detail because my parents had several security guards scattered around the property. But, after Tom's betrayal, I would never make the same mistake again.

Before we reached the top step, the front door flew open, and there stood my mother. One of her security guards must have alerted her of our arrival.

"There is my *fiul*. You have not come to see me in weeks," she chastised me.

She was right; I had not. But she knew how busy I was, especially now with Father gone. Instead of speaking those words, I apologized.

"Sorry, Mother," I said before wrapping her in my arms.

We hugged each other tightly until she was ready to let me go. The fear of losing another loved one caused her to be more affectionate whenever one of us came around. My mother was a strong woman, but losing my father had broken her.

All three of us had pleaded with her to move in with one of us, to keep an eye on her. She refused and told us that she did not want to hear anything else from us on the subject. Roman was the only one she allowed to take care of her, and that was because he was the youngest and the most spoiled. He stayed with Mother for weeks after Father's funeral until Mother told him he had to go home. She told him she needed time alone to heal, and he respected her wishes.

"Good morning, ma'am," Ari greeted my mother.

My mother pulled her into her arms and hugged her just as tightly as she did me.

"Come on in. Breakfast is ready and on the table," she told us.

All four of us followed my mother inside. We all stopped by the bathroom in the hallway to wash our hands before entering the dining room and having a seat. The dining room table was full of food trays that included bread, butter, jam, eggs, vegetables, and cold cuts. She even baked my favorite, *Cozonac*, and we normally only eat it on holidays.

My stomach rumbled, and I reached out to pick up an empty plate from the stack of plates my mother had on the table. Ari reached her hand out and stopped my hand from grabbing it. Confused, I watched as she stood up and grabbed the same empty plate that I was reaching for.

"What all kinds of food would you like on your plate?" she asked me.

It dawned on me that this was our first home-cooked meal together. For the last couple of weeks, we had only eaten take-out food.

"Eggs, salami, bread, and jam. On a separate plate, I want a hefty slice of Cozonac."

Ari smiled and fixed everything I requested. Still confused, I looked at my mother. My mother always brought out all the food and let my father, my brothers, and I fix our own plates. She laughed, clearly amused by my confusion.

Ari set both plates of food in front of me and then proceeded to make a cup of the *Socata* my mother made and put the cup in front of me as well. If I hadn't just watched her fix my food and drink, I would have assumed she was trying to poison me.

"Why are you doing this?" I asked her.

"I'm from Alabama. We are raised to fix our husband's plates of food and drink," she answered.

I made a mental note to ask Alexandur if Kenya did the same for him. Ari sat down and began to fix her own plate.

"Am I supposed to fix your food like you fixed mine?" I asked.

"No, Constatin. Believe it or not, I actually enjoy serving my husband. My mother always fixed my father's plates, and I guess I will be the same."

"Last week, Roman told me your wife took a bat to everything in your house, and now she is fixing your food. You did a good job choosing a wife *fiul* (son)."

"How can you tell?" I asked my mother.

When did destroying property become a good character trait in a wife?

"You need someone who keeps you on your feet, Constatin. A weak woman would only upset you. Elizabeth would have never made you happy."

Hearing Elizabeth's name angered me. It would not be long before she slipped up, and we caught her. The only thing worse than a rat is a backstabbing rat. Killing her was not enough to even the score, but it would have to do.

"Thank you, ma'am. Your son is a mean man, but I know how to be mean too," Ari replied to my mother. She was staring at me with a weird look on her face as she spoke.

Had I said something to upset her?

"Please call me Mother."

Ari turned her gaze away from me and met my mother's eyes. They smiled at each other. My mother's acceptance of my wife was not mandatory, but hearing that she approved of my decision was a great relief.

For the rest of the morning, my mother and Ari bonded over easy conversation. Hours had passed before I told Mother it was time for us to go. On the way out of the front door, my mother hugged us both tightly again.

"Having a husband is a lot like raising a small child. Sometimes, they have to learn lessons the hard way. Stay strong."

She and Ari exchanged a look of understanding between each other before I took Ari by the hand and guided her to the car.

"Where are we going?" Ari asked me five minutes later. She was turned away from me, looking out of the car window as Emet drove.

"Wherever you want."

She turned away from the window to stare at me.

"Hell, anywhere. I have been stuck inside the penthouse for almost a week," she responded.

"Be specific, Ari."

"Hmmmm. Can we go skating?"

I parted my mouth to tell her yes when my cell phone started ringing. The call was from my brother Alexandur. When I answered, he said, "We have a problem," and hung up.

"Emet, take us to the penthouse immediately."

"Yes, sir," he replied.

"I thought we were going skating?" Ari's voice was filled with disappointment.

"Change of plans. I have business to attend to."

Ari rolled her eyes at me before turning her body back toward the window. At the penthouse, I watched Mikey escort my wife inside the building before Emet and I drove away. The penthouse was the safest place for her to be. Mikey would protect her with his life.

On the drive over to my brother's home, I watched Ari on the cameras. She was so upset with me that she was pacing back and forth. A part of me wanted to text her, but I decided against it.

Roman's car was already parked at Alexandur's when I arrived. Emet parked beside it, and I got out. We all owned keys to each other's homes, but Kenya opened the door as soon as I approached. She and I spoke briefly before she pointed toward the kitchen. In Alexandur's kitchen sat Alexandur and Roman.

"What is going on?" I asked, not in the mood for idle chatter.

"Matias is demanding a five percent pay increase, or he isn't sending our normal shipment on schedule," Alexandur replied.

Matias ran the coca farm in Colombia, where we got our cocaine. It was some of the purest cocaine in the world, and we had been in business with the Matias family for years.

"Call the jet and tell them to expect us within the hour. A trip to Antioquia is needed."

Alexandur nodded and pulled out his phone to do as I asked.

The distribution of cocaine was the only illegal activity that the Romanian Mafia dealt in. When my grandfather ran, the times were different in the mafia. The mafia had their hands in everything, from human trafficking and extortion to insurance fraud and prostitution.

In the 1970s, that had changed drastically. The Feds created the *Racketeer Influenced and Corrupt Organization Act* (RICO). They used this act to take down some of the most powerful mafia families in the United States.

All the Feds had to do was to find a rat within a criminal organization, such as the mafia, and get them to snitch. Once the snitch confirmed that they took part in any kind of racketeering crime while part of a criminal organization, the Feds could charge anybody connected to that snitch with a RICO charge, even if that person did not personally commit the crime with the rat.

Once the Feds arrested hundreds of individuals involved in the mafia, using that act, the remaining leaders joined together and created a board. Their job was to decrease the chances of more Mafia families ending up in prison by assigning everyone their own areas and approving all illegal activities for each family.

My father could have chosen to deal in more than cocaine, but with the wine business so successful, it wasn't necessary. Instead, he sought out a coca farm that agreed to produce a large amount of cocaine for us and have it shipped to us every month. He found it in Antioquia, Colombia, with Santos, Matias's father.

The Santos family ran their own coca farm, and he agreed to sell my father 2400 kilos of cocaine every month for $2,000 a brick. Once we received the cocaine, we used our own shipping boats that carried our wine to transport the cocaine out. It was a lucrative business deal because we sold each brick/kilo for $25,000, and we only did wholesale.

A few years ago, Santos got sick with cancer and gave control of the farm to his oldest son, Matias. My father, my brothers, and I all flew out to meet Matias. He then agreed to the same terms we had with his father, and we hadn't had any issues arise until now.

If Matias had reached out to Alexandur and requested a sit-down, we would have arranged the meeting, and I would have agreed to the five percent increase. Because he decided to be disrespectful and withhold our product, we had to fly out and spend two days in Colombia.

Alexandur tortured him for hours until his sickly father found us and begged us to spare his life. I agreed, and we spent the remainder of the time scheduling another boat to come and pick up the cocaine and then watching the cocaine set sea once the boat arrived.

ARI

Constatin dropped me off on Saturday and did not return until late Tuesday night. When I woke up the next morning, he had already gotten up and left for work. Yesterday, it was the same shit. He woke up before I did and didn't come home until I was asleep.

At that point, I felt like Tamia when she said, 'there's a stranger in my house.' The only difference is Tamia's ass could leave her man. My ass would die if I left mine.

All morning, I researched nursing jobs that I could work from home. If I didn't figure out something soon, I was going to die of boredom. It was taking everything in me not to call Constatin and cuss his ass out, but I knew his mean ass was only going to hang up the phone on me.

That was why I decided to go see my husband at his job today. Now, there I was, standing in the kitchen, fixing my husband some lunch to take to him. I had to call Kenya and ask her what Romanian dish I could make in a hurry because I wasn't sure if Constatin liked soul food. She told me to make him some stuffed cabbage rolls, and that's exactly what I did.

I glanced down at the outfit I had on. My breasts were peeking out the top of the white v-cut blouse that I had tucked inside my red high-waisted pencil skirt. The pencil skirt showed every inch of my curvy ass. On my feet were the new Red Bottom heels I purchased, courtesy of the man who had turned my life upside down. Instead of spraying on one of my perfumes, I picked up his Baccarat cologne and sprayed it on me. Smiling, I grabbed his food and my purse before walking out of the penthouse. Mikey stood in front of the door as still as the Statue of Liberty.

"Can you take me to see my husband? I want to surprise him with lunch," I asked him.

Mikey looked at me, confused, before reaching for his phone.

"If you call him, it won't be a surprise. I worked hard on making his lunch. I am sure he would love to eat it while it's hot."

Mikey shook his head from left to right before biting his bottom lip. I could see him debating in his head if my husband would be mad or not. It wasn't until he dropped his shoulders and sighed that I knew he had decided to take me.

"Mr. Bucur is going to kill me, but come on," he muttered.

I gave him a big smile before he turned around and walked toward the elevators. When we walked out of the penthouse complex, and I felt the sun on my skin, I wanted to jump for joy. On the ride to Bucur Wine International, I let my window all the way down to feel the wind blowing against my face.

Mikey parked in the same spot that he parked in the last time we were there and walked around to let me out. This time, when I entered the building, I walked around the metal detectors just like Mikey did, and when we walked past the lady at the front desk, I held my left hand up so that she could see my wedding ring.

Mikey and I got on the elevator, and he pushed the button to take us to Constatin's office floor. My heart was racing, and I felt nervous, but that wasn't going to stop me from accomplishing what I came to do.

"Good afternoon, ma'am," Mikey said to the secretary when we got off the elevator. His voice had changed, and I figured he was scared to see my husband's reaction.

Constatin's office door was open when we reached it, but he wasn't inside. I strolled right on in and walked behind his desk to have a seat in his chair. Mikey shook his head at me and mumbled something under his breath. A few minutes later, my husband and Kofi walked through the door in deep conversation.

"Surprise! I know you forgot all about the wife you had at your home, but she was kind enough to fix you some lunch to eat," I said, referring to myself in third person.

He and Kofi stopped talking. Constatin looked at me and then looked around until he spotted Mikey over in the corner, trying to disappear.

"Why are you here?"

"I do not like wasting my words, Constatin. I just told you I'm here to remind you that you are married and to feed you," I replied.

"Well, that's my sign to get the hell on. If you need me, bro, just hit my line," Kofi spoke on his way out of the office.

"GET OUT!" Constatin yelled.

He didn't say which one of us he was talking to, but Mikey ran out of the room so fast that I was surprised his shoes didn't catch on fire.

"You should have called me or texted me before leaving the penthouse."

The audacity of this man to be mad because I didn't call or text him.

"Constatin, you sent me one text message letting me know you were leaving town, and I did not hear anything else from you for three days. Then, you pop your psychotic ass back up and spend every moment in this damn office while I sit in your penthouse by my damn self. Why the fuck did you marry me if you couldn't handle the responsibility that came with being a husband?"

Yup. I said it.

Constatin's right eye started twitching, and he reached down to pinch the skin on his right arm.

"Exactly. You don't have anything to say. Now, can you please come and have a seat so we can eat these stuffed cabbage rolls I fixed for us?"

He eyed me suspiciously before walking toward his desk. I stood and watched him as he lowered his body into his office chair. Constatin removed the lid on the plate of food and set it aside.

"You take the first bite," he said suspiciously.

I laughed but leaned down beside him to pick up a stuffed cabbage roll and took a big bite. He watched me chew it and swallow it before licking my lips. Instead of putting the rest of the cabbage roll back onto the plate, I put it to his lips.

"Your turn." My voice was lower.

Hesitantly, he opened his mouth and took a bite. I smiled at him and winked.

"Can I sit with you?"

Before he could reply, I pushed his seat back a little and sat in his lap.

"What kind of game are you playing?" he questioned.

"My husband is ignoring me, and I want his attention."

Constatin didn't reply, but I could feel his dick getting hard under me. I wiggled a little on his lap, pretending like I was trying to find a comfortable spot. He grabbed me by my braids and pulled my head back.

"Don't tease me, Ari," he warned.

"Why? What are you going to do about it?"

"Is that why you came here? To get my dick hard? Are you going to let me bend you over my desk like a little slut and fuck you until everyone in the office knows my name?"

"You're the boss. They already know your name. And how do you know that you have what it takes to make me scream?"

Constatin put his face into the crook of my neck and bit me before sucking on the spot he bit me at. A moan slipped from my lips, and I could already feel my lace panties getting wet.

"I don't know if this is a game you are playing or not, but I can't get the taste of your pussy out of my mouth. This is your last chance. If you don't want me to sit you on top of my desk and eat your pussy until you cum in my mouth again, get up and go tell Mikey to take you home."

My husband's voice had gotten deeper, causing a shiver to run through my body.

"It's not fair. You know how I taste, but I don't know how you taste," I whispered.

Constatin bit my neck harder before grabbing my face and turning it around. His lips met mine, and we kissed. Constatin used his tongue and his mouth to make love to my mouth. Our tongues didn't just dance together, they fucked. Constantin's hands went to my breasts. My nipples were hard and straining against my white blouse. He used his fingertips to pinch them so hard that I had no choice but to break our kiss to moan again.

"All week, all I could think about was putting that pretty little pussy of yours in my mouth and making you cum over and over."

"And then what?"

My voice was low and full of desire. Constatin's hands left my breasts, and I felt them sliding up my thighs. He moved slowly as if he was giving me time to change my mind. His right hand reached my pussy first, and I almost fainted when he rubbed his thumb against my clit.

"Damn, your panties are soaked. Take them off and get on top of my desk now."

I had to have the strength of Hercules to shake my head.

"Take your dick out. I want it in my mouth."

Constatin moaned, and it was the sexiest noise I had ever heard. "Get on your knees. Show me how bad you want it."

I slid to the floor in front of him and kneeled on my knees. My husband looked at me with so much fire in his eyes that I could feel myself getting hot from peering into them.

"You put on that tight little skirt and waltzed your little ass in here, smelling just like me, to drive me insane," he mumbled before unzipping his pants. My husband reached into his pants and pulled out his hard dick.

Fuck, I knew his crazy ass was going to be blessed.

His dick was a good eight inches long and thick. He had a vein running from the bottom of his dick to right under his mushroom tip. I leaned my head forward and kissed it.

"Stop teasing me, *regina mea (*my queen). Put my dick in your mouth and swallow."

My pussy was so wet that I could feel the inside of my thighs getting sticky. I moved my lips from the middle of his dick, where I kissed it, to the tip. Slowly, I sucked the tip of his dick into my mouth.

"Fuck, Ari," he groaned before grabbing my hair.

I sucked only the tip for a minute before taking as much of his dick as I could down my throat.

He roughly pushed my head down, and I gagged, letting my saliva coat his dick and balls. Up and down, I moved my head, sucking and slurping his dick until the grip he had on my hair tightened. My hands went to his balls, and I could feel how heavy they were. He was getting ready to fill my mouth with his nut.

"Shit. Swallow every drop," he demanded.

I nodded and continued caressing his balls. He'd moved his hips up, forcing as much of his dick into my mouth as he could, when I grabbed both of his balls and twisted them tight, making sure to dig my nails in them.

Constatin screamed, and I jumped up and ran to the door. I took a quick second to wipe all the saliva from around my mouth before opening the door and rushing out.

"Come on, Mikey. We have to go before he kills us!"

I didn't turn around to see if Mikey listened to me or not, but when I got on the elevator, his ass was right behind me. The elevator door closed, and I hit the button for the lobby so fast I damn near broke it.

Mikey and I made it off the elevator and out the door before my phone rang. I didn't even stop walking to look at it. I had opened my own door and climbed inside when Mikey's phone rang. He looked at me in fear, and I almost felt bad for involving him in my foolishness.

"Ye-ye-yes-yess, sir?" Mikey stuttered when he answered the phone.

Constatin said something, and he nodded as if Constatin could see him.

"Straight the-thee-there," he repeated before taking the phone from his ear to look at it.

My mean ass husband must have hung up the phone on him. My cellphone dinged, alerting me to a text message. With a smile, I dug my phone out of my purse to see if the message was from Constatin.

Evil man: You can run all you want, but I will catch you. And when I do, I am going to shove my dick so far down your throat that you will not be able to talk for a week.

Me: Now, all of a sudden, you know how to use your phone to communicate. Imagine that.

Constatin

It was almost ten at night, and I was just finishing work. I would have been done sooner if thoughts of my wife weren't distracting me. All morning, I had been in and out of meetings, so I couldn't check the cameras at home. If I had, I would have known my wife was on her way here. The trip to Colombia left me with a lot of tasks that I needed to accomplish when I returned to work.

Ari was right to call me out for treating her as if she were invisible. My actions weren't a clear indication of how I felt inside, but my feelings didn't matter. It was my responsibility not only to run a successful international company but also to implement new business ventures that increased the amount of revenue we had coming in. It was my responsibility to be the Nasu of the Romanian mafia and to keep the family safe by all means.

The Gala tomorrow night was being held in the private ballroom of the St. Regis Hotel. All twelve members of the board and their close associates would be in attendance. It was by invite only, and I didn't expect there to be more than a hundred people in total. Even though I had stepped into the role of the Nasu as soon as my father died, it wouldn't be official until tomorrow night.

If I failed to produce an heir within a year, the title could be stripped from me and passed on to one of my brothers. When I married Ari, I decided to let sex happen naturally between us. My plans this weekend were for us to go to the gala on Saturday and to visit family on Sunday. Those plans did not include sucking and fucking the shit out of Ari, but after that stunt she pulled earlier, my ability to fight my desires for her was almost nonexistent.

My balls were sore for almost an hour after she left. But if she thought the pain would make me angry, she was wrong. In fact, I had to rush to the bathroom in my office and stroke my dick up and down until I nutted before I could calm down enough to call her and Mikey. She didn't answer my call, but I didn't expect her to.

When I made it inside the penthouse, I stripped and went into the bathroom to take my shower. After I showered and dried my body off, I climbed into bed naked beside Ari. She looked so peaceful sleeping that I leaned over to place a soft kiss against her lips before picking her body up and placing it on top of mine.

My wife's plan to seduce me and then leave me hanging to teach me a lesson today was a success. But there was no faking her body's natural reaction to me. Her pussy was so wet that her juices coated my thumb as soon as I touched her. The realization that she desired me, even though she was pissed at the way I had been treating her, made me even more determined to show her that I could be a good husband to her.

"Wake up, Ari." I gently shook her. She tried to push my hands away from her, but I was persistent until she opened her eyes.

"Ugh, why am I on top of you? Please tell me you didn't do anything to my body last night."

"All I did was place you on top of me to sleep. But we have a lot planned for today. We have to get up."

"Nooooo. The Gala isn't even until seven tonight. Why are you bothering me?" she whined.

"You and Kenya have a full day of pampering scheduled."

"What kind of pampering?"

She had sat up to ask me the question, no longer interested in staying asleep.

"A full service, whatever that means. Kenya can answer your question better than I can. The service will be done at the St. Regis Hotel, where the event is being held. I booked a suite for us to stay in tonight. Pack yourself a bag with everything you will need. Now, get up. We have to leave here in an hour," I urged her.

"Have you cheated on me?"

Huh? Where in the world did that question come from?

"Ari, the only pussy that will be sliding up and down my dick is yours. Today is not the day for any mind games."

She looked like she wanted to say more, but instead, she nodded.

She didn't really think I was sleeping around, did she?

Ari climbed off me and stood up on the floor to head toward the shower, but my hand caught her wrist to stop her.

"I will not cheat on you, Ari. And if, by some extremely rare chance, I did, I would be man enough to tell you that I dishonored our marriage. I am a busy man. I am a strict man. I am even a dangerous man. But I am not a cheating man. Do you believe me?" I needed to know.

"Yeah, I think I do. Let my wrist go, crazy man. We have a lot to do today, remember?"

Ari used humor to hide her emotions, but I let her wrist go. My emotions for her were changing so rapidly that I didn't have the time to process what any of them meant. If I am honest, I wasn't sure if I even wanted to know.

Ari

"Wait, tell me again what happened?" Kenya asked before bursting out laughing. Constatin wasn't joking when he said we were booked for a full-service pampering day. We had our bodies fully waxed, our backs massaged thoroughly, and our nails and facials done. Now, we both were laid back in recliner chairs, getting our toes scrubbed and painted.

"Girl, it's not even that funny."

"You're right, it's hilarious. I can't believe how long it took for you to tell me. We have been here for hours."

"True, but this is the first time we have had a chance to speak in private. I couldn't tell you that I popped up at my husband's job and sucked his dick like my life depended on it while we were getting waxed or facials. They would have heard me and kicked me out of here."

"Naw. That's not the part I want to hear again, trick. Tell me what you did to his balls and how fast you ran your ass up out of there," she asked, laughing.

I rolled my eyes and shot her ass a bird.

"Okay, okay. On a serious note, how are you and Constatin doing?"

"It's complicated," I said.

"Well, if you ask me, it sounds like you are catching feelings for him."

"That's why I didn't ask you."

Kenya's nosey ass swore she knew everything about me.

She burst out laughing again. This time, she actually had tears rolling down her face from laughing so hard. Meanwhile, I didn't find anything funny.

"You know it's okay to care about him, right? You *are* married to the man," she asked like it was a revelation to me.

"So, do you think I got Stockholm syndrome?"

"No. I think we were taught that love can only be sweet and gentle. That's not the case for everybody. Some love stories are dangerous and obsessive."

"Kenya, I really worry about you. Do you hear the words coming out of your mouth?"

"A year ago, if the roles were reversed, and you were to tell me something like that, I would have thought you were crazy too. It wasn't until I met my monster that I no longer wanted sweet and gentle. Neither of those words apply to my husband. My husband loves me so much that he will kill anybody over me, and I would do the same for him. He treats me like a princess. There isn't anything I want that he wouldn't provide for me. If he can't get it the legal way, he will get it the illegal way. The kind of love we have for each other can only be described as dangerous and obsessive."

"Give me sweet and gentle for two hundred, please, Alex," I joked.

We both laughed, easing some of the tension that came with having a serious conversation.

"Something tells me that a few months from now, you will understand the words coming from my mouth more than you think."

"And that scares the fuck out of me," I honestly said.

Kenya reached out to grab my hand. We held hands as if we were a couple for the rest of the time we spent at the spa. We discussed everything but my marriage to the man that she called *The Mind*.

Kenya, Mikey, and the same guard who was with Kenya at the clothing boutique where we bought our dresses for the gala all escorted me up to the room.

"Makeup and hair will be here soon. I will see you later tonight," Kenya said before giving me a tight hug.

"I love you, best friend," I whispered into her ear before she let me go.

She whispered the words back to me like she had done since we were kids before we both blew a kiss to each other. I stood at the door of the hotel room and watched my best friend and her guard walk away until she was no longer in my sight.

Thirty minutes later, there was a knock at the door. A few seconds passed before Mikey opened the door with two other men.

"Makeup and hair are here. They have been searched, but Constatin wants me in the room while they are here," Mikey informed me.

"Of course he does," I replied and shook my head.

An hour later, I stood in front of the mirror in an emerald green one-shoulder, floor-length lace chiffon dress with sequins. The dress had a split that showed a little of my leg and thigh. On my feet were a pair of Christian Louboutin silver crystal embellished, suede platform pumps.

The makeup artist was a magician with a makeup brush. My face was beat to the *Gods*. He used a light and dark green combination to create a smoky look around my eyes that made me look alluring and seductive. The hair stylist and I decided to twist my braids up into an updo but left a few curled strands hanging around my face.

"If I ever needed proof that God showed favor in my life, all it would take is one glance at my beautiful *regina mea* (my queen), and people would turn green with envy."

Constatin entered the hotel room and almost took my breath away. The man was so handsome that it almost hurt to look at him. I noticed that his limp was becoming less noticeable as more time passed. He walked in a slow stride anyway, as if he owned the world and everyone was on his time.

"Are you a religious man, husband?"

"No, my IQ is too high. Religion is a form of control that rich white men like myself use to rule the world. I do believe there is a higher power, but he wouldn't be interested in a devil like me."

Constatin wrapped his arms around me from behind, and I leaned my body back into his chest. Together, we stared at each other in the mirror, communicating words without talking. We were approaching dangerous territory with each other. It's as if we both were standing in front of a fire, reaching our hands out to touch it. We knew that once our hands connected with the fire, it would burn the hell out of us. But the danger was so enticing that we were willing to hurt ourselves just to have a feel of it.

"What if they don't like me?" I asked him.

"It will be in their best interest to hide their dislike. I have already chosen you as *regina mea* (my queen). Anybody who has a problem with it will die." Constatin's voice was full of anger when he replied.

I turned around and reached up to place a kiss on his cheek to calm him down. My intentions were not to upset him. I wasn't born rich, and even though I knew how to spend his money, I would be lying to myself if I said all this didn't make me feel uncomfortable. Nonetheless, I lifted my head high and joined hands with my husband, ready to stand by his side as he officially became the Nasu of the Romanian Mafia.

Constatin

We entered the gala, and I led Ari to our seats. Only my *famailia* (family) sat at my table. There was Alexandur, Roman, my mother, and Kenya. Security was ordered to stand back but watch us closely. Alexandur's security guard, Tree, was the only one I could spot easily, and that was because the man did not let Kenya out of his sight. It was understandable, though, because she stopped my psychotic ass brother from chopping him and his other security guard up without a valid reason.

All the board members were joined by their wives and close associates at their individual tables. Dinner would be served first before Vincent Castillo would stand and call me forward. Vincent Castillo was the boss of *La Cosa Nostra* and the one who was closest to my father. He was the one who I had contacted to inform him that I was married.

The way the board was set up, each boss was given equal control, and they all had to vote on every decision made. Vincent was the most respected and feared boss on the board, and the others tended to do what he said, even though they would never admit it.

Dinner was a simple five-course meal. I tasted a little of each course, but my attention was more on my surroundings. Ari sat beside me at the head of the table, and I had caught plenty of eyes observing her. She was oblivious to it and caught up in conversation with my mother and Kenya. An hour passed before Vincent finally stood, and everyone in the ballroom silenced.

"Come here, Constatin," his voice rang out, loud and steady. I stood up and leaned down to give my wife a quick kiss on her lips before strolling slowly toward where Vincent stood. The kiss was to convey to everyone in attendance that my marriage was of a serious nature.

When I reached Vincent, he leaned forward and placed a kiss on both sides of my cheeks before patting his hand on my back.

"Turn around and stand before the members of the board."

I turned around and stood beside him as expected.

"A vote has been cast, and a decision has been made. Tonight, we stand in unity to welcome Constatin Bucur as the new Nasu of the Romanian Mafia."

Everyone raised their hands to clap while Vincent signaled for the music to begin.

"Thank you," I told him before we gave each other a quick hug.

People were standing up at their tables, ready to dance, but none of them would move to the dance floor until after my wife and I began our dance.

"*Regina mea* (my queen), may I have this dance?"

Ari nodded her head 'yes' and placed her hand into mine.

I helped her out of her seat and guided her to the dance floor. Within moments, the dance floor filled up, and soft, classical musical played in the background.

Ari and I gently swayed together to the beat of the music. The only step left was for us to conceive a child, but that step no longer seemed like an urgent matter.

"Can I cut in?" I heard.

In front of us stood Leo Amuso. Leo Amuso was the son of Oliver Addams. The Addams ran the UK but were nothing more than petty thieves in my eyes. He had a lot of balls to approach me directly, but tonight was a celebration.

"Yes," I replied and let Ari's hands go.

She looked at me worried, but I gave her a reassuring look. She nodded her head in acceptance, and I moved to the side.

"Brother," Alexandur greeted me.

I glanced around the dance floor and noticed Roman was dancing with Kenya, and mother was dancing with Hero, Alexandur's other bodyguard.

Leo started twirling Ari around the dance floor. He was smiling and laughing at her as they danced. Alexandur had begun talking, but my attention was on my wife when I heard her giggle.

What the fuck?

Vincent walked up beside Alexandur and me.

"Tonight was a success," he said, but I just nodded.

Leo was slowly pulling Ari closer to him than was necessary. My feet remained planted until Leo moved his right hand from above Ari's waist to her lower back. His hand was damn near touching her ass. I saw red immediately. My feet were already in motion when somebody grabbed my hand.

"Not in front of everyone. Wait until I give you the signal. He is to be alive when you are finished," Vincent ordered me.

Without replying, I stalked over to my wife and snatched her from Leo's slimy hands.

"What's wrong?" Ari asked. The smile on her face dropped, and she looked at me, concerned. I guided her back to the table where we had a seat.

"Constatin," my wife called my name, but I had no desire to talk.

"Keep a smile on your face, beautiful. Eyes are on you," my mother said to my wife.

For the first time in my life, I was concerned about the emotions that were showing on my face. Time felt like it had slowed down, and every minute, I sat in agony, trying to control my reactions. Finally, Vincent caught my eye and tilted his head to the right. My eyes followed the direction his head was tilted to see Leo open the door to the hallway of the ballroom where the restrooms were.

"If anything goes wrong, get my wife out of here and go straight to your house," I ordered my mother as I stood.

Roman and Alexandur stood and followed me as I advanced toward the restrooms. My brothers' assistance wasn't needed. They only followed to stop me from killing this motherfucker who had the balls to touch my wife in such as provocative manner.

My hand pushed the restroom door open, and I walked inside. Leo was singing at the urinal while he released his bladder. I heard the bathroom door lock behind me. Leo must have heard it, too, because he stopped singing and looked over his shoulder to see who had locked it.

My fist rammed into his face twice, making him fall to the floor. His bottom lip was already leaking blood. I picked my left foot up and kicked him in the face, splitting his lip more.

"What the fuck? Are you insane?!" Leo cried out on the bathroom floor. He had curled his body into a ball to protect himself from me.

"Yes. I am criminally insane," I replied and then stomped my foot into his back, causing him to uncurl his body and cry out in pain.

I squatted on the floor and spit in his face before pulling my gun out of my jacket and bashing him in the head with it repeatedly. Every time I hit him, I would imagine his filthy fucking hands touching my wife's ass and hit him harder. Blood squirted and leaked from various places on his face and head, soiling my one hundred-thousand-dollar Alexander Amosu Vanquish suit.

"Enough!" Roman stepped up to grab my hand and stop me from bashing his head in any further. Roman grabbed my gun from my hand and leaned down over Leo's unconscious body to check his pulse.

"He is barely hanging on. You have taught him his lesson, brother. We must go."

Roman spoke rationally.

Do it. Do it. Do it.

My mind was telling me to take the little life he had left in him but now was not the time.

"Alexandur, give me your knife."

"You know, it would be easier for you to purchase your own knife to carry around with you," Alexandur replied, but he reached into his pocket and pulled his knife out like I asked.

He did not know just how dangerous it would be for me if I were to always have a knife on me. Which is why I only carried a gun on my waist and a gun strapped to my leg.

I reached out to pull Leo's left hand toward me and then put my foot on top of it to hold it still.

"Fuck. Alexandur, stop him!" Roman urged.

"No. I like watching him come unglued. It is a rare sight. You might want to go get medical help, though. Because if he is about to remove any body parts, it won't take Leo long to bleed to death," Alexandur replied.

"Vincent said he can't die!"

"Well, you need to go tell Vincent that our brother is in here playing doctor, and if he wants Leo to live, he had better find a real one."

My brothers continued to converse while I used the knife to cut through Leo's skin on his wrist, then through the bone and cartridge, severing the radial and ulnar arteries. As long as he got medical attention quickly to stop all that blood from pouring out of his body, he would live. He was already unconscious, dropping the chances of him dying from shock. If I elevated his arm above his head and made a tourniquet, it would raise the chances of his survival tremendously.

"Bring my wife to me," I looked up to tell Alexandur before picking up Leo's severed hand and standing up.

Alexandur chuckled and turned around to do as I asked. On his way out of the restroom, Roman and Vincent came rushing in.

"I knew you would pass the test, Constatin. But did you have to make such a mess?" Vincent asked as he glanced at the bloody mess I made of Leo.

Roman and I looked at him in shock.

"Test?" I asked him.

"A few members of the board thought your marriage came with an expiration date, and you know how we frown upon divorce. I disagreed, but you know how things go."

"And if I hadn't reacted at all?"

"You would have found your wife dead in the morning and your title stripped," he stated simply.

In the mafia world, arranged marriages were common as long as both parties understood that the marriage would be for life. If someone thought I had made a marriage arrangement with a time limit on it, they would see it as a sign of disrespect.

"Thanks for the gala. I enjoyed myself," I told him.

Ari and Alexandur were waiting for me when I walked out of the bathroom.

"Constatin, what did you do?" Ari asked.

"Here." I handed her the severed hand.

Ari

I know this isn't a real human hand.
 Omg. Omg. OMG!
 My husband watched me as I dropped the hand on the floor with a disinterested look on his face. He took off his suit jacket and shirt and handed them to his brother.

"Put this on." Alexandur took his suit jacket off and gave it to his sick ass brother.

"Security is standing outside the ballroom, waiting for you two. They won't let anybody get close enough to see the blood spatters on you. Roman and I will handle clean up."

"Pull all the cameras and destroy them."

Alexandur nodded.

Constatin reached his hand out for me to give him my hand. I put both of my hands behind my back.

"I can't do this, Constatin. Nothing about this is okay. You cutting people's hands off and shit in the middle of a party. Then, why the fuck would you hand it to me? That ain't have shit to do with me!" I cussed.

"Every time you let a man touch you, I will cut their hand off and give it to you. Come on, before anyone else comes out of the ballroom."

Wait, what?! Who touched me?

Constatin reached out to grab my arm and pulled me through the side door. Emet and Mickey crowded around us as he dragged me to the elevator.

The elevator ride was silent. I watched the numbers as they climbed and prayed.

God, please don't let this be my last day on Earth. You brought this man into my life. Can you control your experiments, please?

The elevator dinged, and I opened my eyes back up. Constatin tried to reach for my arm again, but I moved out of his reach. He narrowed his eyes at me before walking off the elevator and to the suite he booked. I followed him, mentally preparing myself for some bullshit.

I wonder if this is how Beyoncé felt when she got off that elevator with Jay-Z and Solange.

When he reached the suite, he swiped the card to unlock it and then walked inside. Emet and Mikey stood beside the door on each side. They both watched me as I walked into the suite. The door closed behind me, and my stomach dropped.

The room was still dark. I was walking over to the wall to hit the light switch to turn them on when my husband grabbed me by my neck and slammed me into the wall.

"You do not smile or laugh at other men!" he yelled.

I was trying to shake my head 'no' to tell him I didn't when the dance I had with that guy crossed my mind.

Did he cut that man's hand off for dancing with me? I didn't even want to dance with him in the first place until Constatin gave me the okay.

He squeezed my neck tighter, and I felt myself getting light-headed. Constatin nuzzled his face into my neck and bit me. If I had enough oxygen to breathe, I would have screamed.

"*Regina mea* (my queen), nod your head if you understand."

I quickly nodded my head up and down. He let my neck go, and I slid to the ground and cried.

"Stop crying, Ari. You knew better."

"Fuck you. You told me to dance with him and then choked me because we danced. Yo' ass gon' burn in hell!"

"The moment his hand went from your waist to your ass, you should have pushed him away from you. Instead, you're swirling around, smiling and laughing like you do not belong to me. Do you belong to me, Ari?"

Hell Nawwwwwwww!

"Yes," I sniffled out.

It was still dark in the room, but I heard Constatin approach me. He leaned down to pick me up and carried me to the bedroom.

"Do you want me to make you feel better?" he asked.

I know the answer should have been 'no,' but like a moth to the flame, I said, "Yes."

Constatin

I exhaled the breath that I was holding when Ari said 'yes.' My face lowered to hers, and I kissed her softly. Our tongues mated together erotically. The kiss deepened, and I sucked on her tongue while my hands roamed her body. Ari moaned into my mouth. I bit her bottom lip before breaking the kiss.

I held my hand out to help her stand up, and then I turned her around to unzip her dress. Her dress hit the floor before I guided her back to the bed to sit while I bent down on my knees to remove her heels. All Ari had left on her body was an emerald lace bra and matching emerald lace panties.

My dick was swollen inside my pants, excited to finally get what he had been craving for weeks. I was not rushing tonight, though. I would spend hours, if that's what it took, to make sure I pleased Ari's body the way it deserved to be pleased.

Quickly, I stood back up and removed all my clothes and my shoes. The possibility that I still had some of Leo's blood splattered on my body made what we were about to do even more exhilarating. I pushed Ari's body on top of the bed, getting on my knees to put my face in her pussy.

"I cut a man's hand off tonight for touching you. If I had my way, I would have killed him for making you laugh. Does that turn you on? Knowing that I want you so much that I will kill anybody to have you? What does it feel like, knowing you have other people's lives in your hands?"

My wife did not answer, but she did not have to. The inside of her thighs was sticky with her arousal. I lifted her left leg up slightly, using my tongue to clean her nectar before doing the same to her right leg.

"Look at me while I eat your pussy."

I waited until Ari raised her upper body, our eyes connecting before I began. I dragged my tongue from the bottom of her pussy up, pausing to lightly suction her clit on each pass. I did this a few times before focusing only on her button. Now, going between light suctions and soft flicks of my tongue on her clit, then sliding the middle and pointer fingers of my right hand inside of her. I finger fucked her tight, snug, and warm pussy while still licking on and sucking her clit until my fingers were soaked and her legs were shaking. I made sure to wrap my left arm around her inner thigh to lock her in place. Then I removed my two fingers from her pussy's grip for a moment to lead a trail of her juices down to her asshole. I used my thumb to lubricate and stimulate her puckered hole.

"What are you doing?" she asked me.

Instead of answering, I kept licking and sucking her clit. Then, I plunged my fingers back into her pussy with my inner wrist facing down instead of up, so I could also hook my thumb in her asshole with the same hand. I plunged both in and out at a steady pace, fingers pumping and twisting and massaging her from the inside out.

"Aahhhhhhhhhh!" Ari screamed a few minutes later before erupting all over my face. I didn't stop, though. My fingers continued their assault while I continued to latch onto her clit like a newborn latched onto a tit.

"Stop. Stopppp..." she begged me.

I increased the speed of my finger plunges, slamming them into her pussy and asshole harder. Her body began to tremble. She reached down to try to push my head away, but I wasn't budging.

"OHHHH, MY GODDDD!" Ari cried. She was still propped up. Her upper body seized until her midsection started jerking, and warm liquid shot out of her. I stopped then and grabbed her hips to lift her up before trying to dive my whole face into her pussy. My control was gone. I groaned while eating and sucking on her pussy like it was the last meal I would have before execution.

"Please. Please..." Ari weakly begged me.

I did not want to stop eating her pussy yet, but that was selfish thinking. So, I stood and pulled her body to the edge of the bed. My dick lined up with her pussy, and I slowly slid inside her, letting her feel every inch of my dick as I stretched her pussy out.

"Fuck. I thought I was just obsessed with the taste of your pussy. But the way she is gripping my dick while flooding like this is insane. Damn, girl. Why is your pussy so good?"

Ari was moaning loudly.

I rocked back and forth inside her before lifting both of her legs and putting them over my shoulders. Ari lifted her hips and started fucking me back. The plans I had to fuck her slowly faded quickly, and I began to pound into her. This wasn't lovemaking. This was fucking in its rawest, most natural and animalistic form. My hand found its own way between her thighs to rub circles on her clit.

"Yess, yess..." she chanted. Her pussy gripped my dick even tighter, making my toes curl involuntarily.

"Fuck, Ari. Cum on my dick so I can give you these babies," I moaned.

Ari stopped fucking me back, froze for a minute, and then she screamed. She was cumming so much that we were going to have to change the sheets.

My vision was blurry, and my nose flared as nut shot out of my dick, straight into her pussy. I pushed my dick as deeply as it could go, still pumping while trying to spread my nut everywhere. I wanted to make sure her pussy knew that I was claiming my territory.

"Wake up, *regina mea*."

I shook Ari's shoulders until she groaned. I knew she was tired because after we fucked for the first time, we took a shower, changed the sheets, and fell asleep in each other's arms. It was almost checkout time, though, and the jet was scheduled to take off in an hour.

"We have family to visit today. Get up."

She whined but opened her eyes to look at me. Ari was breathtakingly gorgeous. Her hair was out and flowing all over the pillow. Her smooth, peanut butter skin always looked like it had a glow. She hadn't even fully opened her eyes yet, but I was still mesmerized.

"Are we having brunch with your mother today?" she asked.

"No, we are having lunch with your mother today."

Ari rubbed her eyes and started laughing. I let her laugh for a few minutes before interrupting her.

"You know, I don't do jokes. I'm serious."

She stopped laughing and sat up in bed. She stretched her arms out wide before responding to my statement.

"How are we supposed to go to Alabama to visit my mother today by lunchtime? And why would we be going?"

"We are going on my father's jet. It is only a forty-five minute flight from Atlanta to Alabama, where your mother is. As far as why we are going, it is because she's family, and you are supposed to spend time with family."

That's not the whole truth, but it is the truth.

"Can we reschedule?"

For some reason, Ari looked scared. I squinted my eyes at her, and she turned her head to avoid my gaze.

"We have been married for over a month now. You did tell your mother you were married, right?"

"Yeah, no. I haven't really gotten the chance to tell her yet,"

"Do not lie to me! Do not worry about it, though. We will tell her together *today*."

My wife looked like she wanted to argue, but there was nothing she could say that was gonna stop us from going to visit her mother today. Today was the only day that I would be able to fly out for the next few weeks because of my schedule.

An hour and ten minutes later, Ari and I boarded the jet.

Ari

My Mama is gonna kill my black ass! Well, at least I got to experience what other women meant when they say they got their brains fucked loose. Last night, the little string of common sense I was clinging to was gone bye-bye. If my mama didn't kill me, trying to figure out what I was gonna do about the complicated man I married would.

Constatin opened the back passenger door for me and held his hand out to help me out of the car. I got out, and we walked hand in hand toward an all-white jet with G50 on the back wing in blue. Emet and Mikey followed closely behind us.

Standing at the top of the flight of stairs was an older white lady with red hair that she had pulled back in a bun. She had on a yellow blouse with a white skirt and white heels. Beside her was a white male with grey hair. He looked older than the flight attendant, but not by more than a few years. He wore a red polo shirt and some blue jeans. They both greeted us as we boarded the plane.

"Hey," I responded to them both and smiled.

"What kind of jet is this?" I asked as Constatin led me to a second row of brown leather seats. Of course, this was my first time flying private, and it surprised me how spacious it was.

"It's a Gulf Stream G650. It can carry eleven to eighteen passengers at one time. There's a small bed in the back and a bathroom. Right there is a bar stocked full of bottled water, sodas, and a few alcoholic beverages. If you are hungry, the flight attendant keeps snacks and easy-to-make meals on hand," Constatin detailed.

"Thanks," I replied and turned to look out of the closest small jet window.

I had only flown commercial a couple of times, and both times, I ended up stuck in the middle seat. On this flight, I planned to gaze at the blue sky and the fluffy white clouds.

"Tell me about your parents," my husband requested.

"My mother and I are close. She is a nurse. She works third shift in the local nursing home. Um... she can be opinionated, like me. I guess that's it."

Opinionated was putting it nicely. Mom said whatever came to her mind.

"Ari, take off won't happen for another five minutes or so, and even then, Phil will announce it on the intercom. Why are you staring out of the window instead of looking at me?"

I turned away from the window to look at him like he wanted. His eyes scanned my face, but I kept my face blank.

"Happy?"

"If you had not squirted all over my face and covered my dick with your cum, I would have thought I did not please you right last night, and that is why you are acting closed off and secretive. But that is obviously not the case. So, what is the issue?"

My mouth dropped open, and I leaned over to hit him in the arm. Emet and Mikey had chosen to sit in the far back and didn't hear what Constatin had just said. I looked around for the flight attendant, but I couldn't spot her.

"There isn't any issue. I just don't like having to lie to my mother. That's why I haven't spoken to her much because we have a very honest relationship."

Constatin shrugged as if he still couldn't see the issue.

"Tell her the truth, then. I do not see the problem."

Yeah, 'cause clearly yo' momma didn't whoop any of y'all asses as kids. That's why y'all insane in the brain now.

"You want me to tell my mother that I am married to a billionaire who is also a mafia boss. She is going to kill me. Ohhh, and let's not forget that I quit my job. My ass is grass!"

Constatin threw his head back and laughed. I think, over the last month, I had only heard him laugh three times. A smile tugged at my lips, and I had to fight hard to control it.

"How about we answer the questions together? I am quite intelligent," he proposed.

No comment.

"Hey, it's your funeral."

I turned back toward the window, hoping that ended our conversation. But, sadly, I was wrong.

"Tell me about your father?" he asked.

I closed my eyes and took a few deep breaths. This conversation was quickly heading in a direction that I didn't want it to go in.

"No," I replied, hoping he could tell from my harsh answer that I did not want to talk about my father.

"Why?"

None of your business!

"My father is not a topic I like to discuss."

Please drop it.

"We are married. We discuss all topics. I know he is in prison for life on a murder charge. Is that why you don't want to talk about him? Do you hate him?"

I opened my eyes and turned away from the window again to glare at him. My right leg had started to shake.

"Keep my daddy's name out of your mouth. That man is my Superhero. He gave his life to protect me, and I don't take kindly to people talking about him when they don't know what the fuck they are talking about!"

Constatin reached forward and wiped a tear from my face. That's why I didn't like discussing my father. I got too emotional, and I couldn't control it. It took me a few minutes to calm down. Constatin waited patiently, reaching forward to wipe my tears a couple more times.

"Tell me," he softly said. I could tell from the look in his eyes that he wasn't going to let it go.

"As you know, I am an only child. My parents worked hard to provide for me, which sometimes meant they had to ask friends or family to watch me. My father was a truck driver for a local company. He tried hard to be home every day, but sometimes, he would get sent to take a load to Georgia or Florida. Anyway, long story short, my uncle had moved in with us. He needed a place to stay, and he didn't mind helping to watch me whenever my parents were at work. He practically helped raise me whenever he wasn't in prison or jail, and we were really close.

"My twelfth birthday came, and my parents threw me a birthday party, which later turned into an adult party. I had gone to bed at around nine and was asleep when I heard my room door open in the middle of the night. At first, I thought I was dreaming because I didn't hear anything else. But a few minutes later, I heard a male voice groaning. I opened my eyes, and my uncle was standing over my bed with his penis in his hand, jacking off. He had his eyes closed, and he didn't know I saw him. Scared, I closed my eyes back and pretended to be sleeping. He did the same thing four nights in a row, and each night, the experience was worse. He would whisper my name and ejaculate on my pillow next to my head.

"I know you are wondering why I didn't tell anybody, but it was because my uncle was known for fighting and assaulting people. He wasn't like my father. My father never, ever even raised his voice at me. I was scared that if I told, he would hurt my daddy, so I didn't say anything. In the end, it didn't matter.

Because on that fourth night, my father came home and caught him. Before my uncle could try to explain, my daddy started fighting him. My room was dark, and everything was happening so fast.

"I remember yelling out for my uncle not to hurt my daddy. My dad was the one who hurt my uncle, though. In the middle of their fight, my dad picked up the wooden clock I used to have on my dresser and hit my uncle in the head with it. My uncle ended up falling and never getting back up. My dad did the right thing and called the police, but he was still arrested. I told them what happened. They made me come to the jailhouse and questioned me again, and I told them the exact same truth. My mother took all of her money out of her savings and hired a cheap lawyer. When it was time for court, the judge agreed with the prosecution that my father's actions were violent and my uncle's death was intentional. My daddy was found guilty of murder and got life. I haven't seen or spoken to him since. He refuses to see me or talk to me because he says that he doesn't want me to do the time with him since I didn't do anything wrong."

"I am sorry that you had to go through that," Constatin replied when I finished telling him. He reached out again to hold my face in his hand.

"Don't feel pity for me. My father did what he did to protect me. In high school, I knew a girl who was getting raped by her older brother. Her parents knew about it, too, but they looked the other way because he was paying all of their bills. The girl got pregnant, and they forced her to abort the baby, scared that it would get out, what they had allowed to happen. A few days after she had the abortion, the girl killed herself. Believe it or not, what happened to me and the girl I met in high school were not uncommon stories. Most Black people, especially the older generations, are raised not to tell on their own family and to keep their problems in the home. I would never raise my child like that. I feel so bad for all the kids who were abused and the people who were supposed to protect them, didn't. If I could, I would wrap my arms around them tight and tell them that what happened to them wasn't their fault and that they did nothing wrong. And I pray they find a way to heal one day because depression kills, and they deserve to live a good life, just like everyone else. That's why I call my father 'My Superhero,' because he saved my life."

The pilot's voice came over the intercom, announcing that we were about to take off. I sat back in my seat, all buckled in and turned my head back toward the window. Constatin had reached over to grab my hand. He held my hand the whole flight to Alabama and didn't let it go until it was time for us to land.

Constatin

The jet landed in Troy, Alabama, at their airport. Like most airports, a landing fee had to be paid for using their airstrip, but I paid extra to leave the jet for a few hours until we returned. The driver I hired to drive us around was standing with a white sign that had Bucur written in black marker on it. While holding *regina mea's* (my queen) hand, I guided us toward the driver. She was still quiet after the deep conversation we'd just had. I had texted Kofi and told him to pull her father's case and see what could be done about it.

The driver guided us to a black 2024 Ford Expedition that was parked in front of the airport. He walked around and opened the doors for everyone before getting in the driver's seat. Ari gave him her mother's address, and he entered it into his GPS on the dashboard before pulling off. If we weren't on a time restriction, I would have rented us a vehicle and had it waiting for us in the airport parking lot, but we were only staying long enough for me to meet my mother-in-law and for us to converse. The ride to her mother's house was a silent one. We passed a lot of farms with cows and horses in their yards until he turned onto a highway that led us to the two-bedroom home that Ari's mother lived in.

"Let me do most of the talking," Ari said when we pulled in

front of a small light blue house with a dilapidated wire fence around it.

In the driveway was a red Buick Lasabre that I knew from my background check belonged to her mother. The driver got out of the car and opened the doors again for everyone.

Ari had tightened her grip on my hand, but I did not believe she knew she had done it. My feelings for her worried me. She had the power to break me, and unlike Elizabeth's betrayal, I knew I would not be able to survive without her.

"Is that my baby?" I heard an older woman yell.

Her voice had a deep Southern accent. The front door of the house swung open and out rushed a woman who didn't look a day older than thirty. The woman ran to Ari, and Ari dropped my hand to wrap her arms around her.

"I missed you, Momma," Ari told the woman, confirming that she was indeed her mother. When they finally separated, her mother took her time looking at each one of us before looking back at her daughter.

"Now, I know I was born at night, but it damn sure wasn't last night, right?" she said to Ari.

I hadn't the slightest idea what she meant, but Ari did because she quickly shook her head from left to right.

"No, ma'am. You wasn't born last night," Ari muttered. Now, her voice had a deep Southern accent to it, too.

"Little girl, you got about three seconds to tell me why you got that big ass ring on your marriage finger? Who the hell is that fine ass man staring at you like a piece of meat? Last, but damn shole not least, why you got the Men in Black following you around like you are Madam President of the United States?"

"Momma, we need to talk. I think it's best we go inside and have a seat."

"Hmmmm," she replied before turning around and going back inside the house.

We followed her to the door.

"Stay," I told the guards and followed Ari into her mother's house.

"Did that man just tell them other grown ass men to stay like a puppy, and they listened?" Ari's mother asked her.

She was sitting on a miniature burgundy-colored couch. Ari sat down right beside her. Her living room was smaller than my closet at the penthouse, and that just wasn't acceptable.

"Mom! I can't believe that you are being so rude. And they are security guards. Their job is to protect us."

"See, now I got more questions because who the hell is *us,* and why does *us* need protection?" she asked.

I felt like I was missing half of the conversation. Ari stared at her mother, clearly frustrated. That was my cue to step in.

"Ma'am, I am your son-in-law. Your daughter and I have been married for a little over a month. She is scared to tell you that she had to quit her job for safety reasons, but I am a billionaire, and I take care very good care of her. Oh, and the reason why I flew her out here to have lunch with you wasn't just because we needed to meet, even though I am honored to be in your presence. It was also to inform you that you have to move. But I am here to provide you with the assistance you need."

Ari and her mother both stared at me with matching looks of bewilderment on their faces. I thought they looked similar before, but now that they were sitting beside each other, they looked like twins.

"Excuse me, sir. I think I might have forgotten my manners. I am Annie B., but you can just call me Annie. What is your name, sir?"

"Constain Legion Bucur," I replied.

"So, put Ari and Constain Bucur on your headstones, correct?"

"Well, no. We are getting buried in coffins and pushed into the sea," I informed them both.

"What the fuck? Constain, if my momma don't kill you, I am when we get back on your jet!" she fussed at me.

"Our jet, *regina mea*. Ours," I corrected her. As the oldest son, it belonged to me, but I still refer to it as my father's.

"Ari, I know this is some kind of joke. Are y'all two really married? Did you two have a courthouse wedding?" She was looking back and forth between her daughter and me. Ari was looking at me and shaking her head no, but I had not asked her any questions.

"The papers were filed at the courthouse, yes, but I filed them by myself. Ari was not aware that we were legally married until later that night."

"Lord Jesus," Ari muttered.

Ari's mother jumped up from her couch and ran to the back of her house. I knew it wouldn't take long for her to return. Ari jumped up and ran to stand in front of me.

Why is everybody running?

My mother-in-law returned with a sawed-off shotgun and pointed it right at my head.

"Ma. Put that gun down, now!" Ari yelled at her.

Emet and Mikey ran in with their weapons drawn. It was a very intriguing sight.

"Lower," I ordered.

My security guards complied and lowered their weapons. My mother-in-law did not comply and kept her sawed-off shotgun aimed at my head.

"Mother-in-law, this is all very intriguing, but we really have to discuss this half-a-million-dollar check that I brought for you and your new home. My schedule is full for the next few weeks, and it's not safe for you here." I informed her.

"Half a million dollars!?" Ari and her mother screamed at me.

At the same time, my mother-in-law lowered her weapon, but she didn't run to put it back up.

"I thought you were yanking my leg when you said you were a billionaire, son." Finally, she smiled at me, and I think we had just received her blessing.

My security guards went back outside. I explained to her that the half a million dollars was for her and that I would pay for the home she moved into, but it had to be in a gated community with strict security. A few hours later, Momma Annie had fed us good and sent us on our way.

Ari

There was never a dull day with my husband. I just knew my momma was going to blow his head off. But she lowered that gun quick when he mentioned giving her half a million dollars.

Constatin didn't even tell me we were going to give my mother money. All he said was that we were eating lunch. He confused the hell out of me. One minute he was cold, and the next, he did the sweetest shit.

My mother pulled me aside and asked me if I was really okay with him. After I confirmed I was, she told me that God gave me baby-making hips for a reason and to use them. My mom had no chill, but I loved that about her. Constatin told her we would be back to visit soon, and I hoped we would. It was dark in Atlanta when we stepped off the Jet. Now, we were in the back seat of Emet's car on the way to the penthouse.

"The contractors are done removing all the items from the mansion. Do you want to keep it as a second home or put it on the market? I also need a list sent to me of the requirements you have and recommendations you want for the new home. My realtor will begin a search for our new home next week. I am tired of staying at the penthouse."

Hmmm. I honestly don't have any special requirements; I just want to decorate my own home.

"Why can't we just move back into the mansion you already own instead of wasting millions on a new home?"

"One would assume you had a dislike for that home," he retorted.

"No. I actually enjoyed staying there, but it's up to you. I have no special requirements other than I want to decorate my own home."

"If you want to move back into the mansion, I see no problem with it. Mikey can take you over there tomorrow for a walk-through. Just let me know when items such as our bedroom set and kitchen appliances are scheduled to be delivered. We can move in then."

I nodded instead of responding, excited and ready to start shopping. Neither of us said anything else during the remainder of the ride. Both of us focused on our phones until the car stopped.

When we entered the penthouse, fatigue was hitting me fast.

"I'm going to take my shower," I told Constatin before heading into the closet to get something to wear to bed.

When I exited the closet, I walked straight into the bathroom and turned the shower on before removing my clothes. A few minutes later, I stood under the shower head, letting the hot water cascade down my naked body before I started to scrub my body clean.

"You are so beautiful," Constatin whispered into my ear, scaring the shit out of me.

"I didn't hear you come in," I replied and leaned my body back against his chest.

His dick was hard, and I could feel every inch of it pressed against my ass.

"Get on your knees. I want my dick down your throat."

I turned around toward him and lowered to my knees like he asked. My pussy contracted, and a warm sensation flowed through my body. Both of my hands reached out to pick his dick up before I opened my mouth and spat on it. Slowly, I stroked up and down his dick with my hands while looking him in his eyes.

"Be a good little whore and swallow my dick, Ari," he whispered. His voice was darker than normal. I stopped stroking his dick and moved my face closer to suck his balls into my mouth, one by one.

"Yes," he moaned.

I went back and forth, licking and sucking on his balls, making sure to let some of my saliva flow out of my mouth and down to his gooch. I stopped sucking his balls and leaned my head back to put his dick in my mouth. Without using my hands, I slowly sucked every inch of his dick down my throat. I kept going until my throat tightened from having something stuck in the middle of it. Constatin grabbed a handful of my braids and roughly moved my head up and down, fucking my face. My right hand slid between my legs and massaged my clit, while my left hand went under his ball sack and rubbed his gooch.

"Shit. You're a nasty bitch," he growled, shoving his dick down my throat harder.

"Ummmm," I moaned, my cum leaking down my legs as I came.

"Ohhh, FUCKKKKK!" Constatin gasped before filling my mouth with so much nut that some dripped out of my mouth and slid down my chest.

Constatin reached down and grabbed me by my neck, pulling me up to my feet. He turned me around and shoved my body into the shower wall before I felt his hands grab both of my ass checks and spread them wide.

The feeling of his thick, pink tongue licking from the bottom of my ass to the top had my body bucking and my eyes closing.

"You swallow my dick so good. You deserve to have your ass ate," Constatin said before sliding his tongue inside my asshole.

Tears gathered in my eyes from the intense feelings of ecstasy flowing through my body. In and out, his tongue went, flicking inside my asshole until I cried out. A gush of warm liquid shot from inside me and down my legs.

I struggled to catch my breath. My second orgasm caused my body to erupt with so much pleasure I felt weak. Constatin stood up and picked my body up. I could still hear the shower running in the background before he laid me down on the bed.

Constatin climbed on top of me and used his legs to spread

my legs apart. He pushed his dick inside me, filling my pussy up. Constatin grinded his dick into me, rolling his hips so his dick grazed my clit on every plunge.

"I can't do it," I stuttered.

The pleasure my body experienced was too much. There was no way my body could handle cumming again.

"You belong to me. I will kill you before I let anybody else have you," he warned me out of thin air.

Constatin stopped grinding in and out of me and began to fuck me slowly. My body was too weak to fuck him back. All I could do was lie there and take it.

"Tell me who you belong to, Ari."

Constatin increased his thrusts, pounding into my pussy with his big-ass demonic dick.

"Babyyy. Please," I begged. My stomach was tightening, and the pleasure was turning into a searing hot pain because it was so intense.

"Tell me you will have my baby, and I will let you cum."

"Fuck. Okay... okay, I will have your baby. Just stop!" I yelled, tears flowing down my cheeks.

Constatin reached down to pinch my clit, and my body immediately erupted into a million pieces.

"Shit," he spread my legs wider, shoving his dick so far inside me that I knew my pussy was going to be sore tomorrow.

"*Te iubesc, regina mea,*" he repeatedly whispered into my ear until I felt his warm nut shoot inside me.

Constatin

WIFE: I have ordered almost all the big items and scheduled them for delivery next Wednesday.
ME: We can start moving next weekend. I miss you.
Wife: I miss you, too.
Me: I will be home late. Got a lot of paperwork.
Wife: Okay.

Lying to my wife was not something I did frequently. But, I did not want to inform her of where I was and get her hopes up prematurely. I would wait until the situation had a clear path to a resolution.

I slid my phone inside my suit's inner pocket and let myself out of the back door of Emet's truck. Then, I walked around the back to the passenger side door and opened it for Mrs. Dorval. Mrs. Dorval was one of the best criminal attorneys in Atlanta, who also had licenses to practice in both Alabama and Florida.

Mrs. Dorval got out, and we both walked together toward the Bibb County Correctional Facility in Brent, AL. Emet could not come inside with us, but he would remain outside until we returned.

The inside of the prison was cold, and the paint on the walls was chipping from the lobby on. Mrs. Dorval walked up to the glass window where a female correctional officer sat, typing on her computer.

"Who you here for?" the correctional officer asked. The woman's eyes remained on the computer screen the whole time she talked.

"Our client is named Joe Taylor," Mrs. Dorval answered.

The correctional officer nodded before picking up a black walkie-talkie and telling someone to take inmate number 00238765 to the visitation room for a meeting with his lawyers. When she finished, she put the walkie-talkie down and went right back to typing.

Mrs. Dorval stepped aside and turned toward a grey steel door. A few minutes later, I heard a clinking noise, and the door opened. The sounds on the other side of that door were deafening.

"Come on," a male officer called us forward.

Mrs. Dorval and I approached the man. She spread her arms out wide, and he used a metal detector to scan her for weapons. When he finished, he did the same to me before turning around and walking away. Mrs. Dorval followed him, and we walked through the prison to another door that was closed. The correctional officer opened the door. Mrs. Dorval thanked the man, and we walked inside to have a seat at the tacky brown round table in the middle of the room. My suit would be thrown away when I left this filthy ass building.

The correctional officer returned a few minutes later with a big, tall, muscular black man in an orange jumpsuit. He was bald-headed with the same peanut butter complexion as Ari. That was the only similar feature they had that I could see, but I was not surprised. Ari had every single one of her mother's features. Ari's father was led to the seat across from us. Once he had a seat, the officer turned around and walked back out of the room.

"Who are y'all?" Ari's father asked after the door had closed completely. His voice was deeper than I expected, but he had the same deeply southern accent as his wife.

"I am your son-in-law," I replied.

His eyes widened before he looked me up and down and then chuckled.

"You the one who got the Men in Black?" he asked.

I chuckled then and relaxed a little.

"Mama Annie told you about me?"

He smiled when I mentioned her name. Ari did not mention if her parents were still together or not, but it was obvious they still communicated frequently.

"Something like that. I know she didn't say anything about you being a lawyer."

"I am not, but Mrs. Dorval is your attorney."

He frowned then and shifted his glance to look Mrs. Dorval over before turning back to look at me.

"No disrespect, but I would rather talk about my daughter. Are you good to her?"

"I think so. Marriage is harder than I realized, but we are happy."

At least, I think we are.

"Are you ready to see your daughter?" I inquired.

A grimace crossed his face. I had wondered if the reasons that he didn't want to see his daughter were honest. Now, I could clearly see that he was doing what he thought was right, regardless of how much it hurt him. If Ari's uncle wasn't already dead, I would enjoy torturing him for weeks before squeezing the little life out of him that he had left.

He chucked again, but this time, it was more of a sarcastic chuckle.

"I got about thirteen more years before I qualify for parole. I'm good as long as my baby girl is good." He tilted his head to the side and glared at me.

He was threatening me without threatening me.

"Tomorrow, news is going to break that the 'Honorable'

Judge Grandville is being investigated for unethical practices. All of his cases from 2010-2013 are going to be reopened. Your case will be one of the first because your attorney will be filing a court motion to have you released immediately. A court date will then be set for a judge to hear the case and decide if we have a valid reason for the motion."

He was quiet at first, just silently studying me. I let him because whether he liked it or not, we were *familia*. It took him a few minutes to process what I had just said.

"The evidence you have must be good, because I definitely committed the crime that I am in here for."

"No. You should have never been charged with more than manslaughter. If you had a good attorney back then, you would not have been charged at all."

"Don't tell my baby girl. I don't wanna get her or my hopes up. But, if things do go as you say, I would like to surprise her."

"I agree," I replied.

We spent another twenty minutes in the visitation room. Miss Dorval explained to him more about why he was found guilty of murder. The judge over his case was having an affair with the prosecutor. Every case the prosecutor brought before the judge somehow turned into all guilty verdicts.

It went on for three years until the prosecutor quit her job with the state and moved an hour away. She got a job with a smaller local firm. Kofi found evidence that not only were they having an affair, but they had a child together.

When the prosecutor got pregnant, she moved an hour away, and they gave the little boy her last name. The judge messed up, though, because he still signed the birth certificate, assuming that no one would find out.

Once Mrs. Dorval presented all the supporting evidence that we had gathered, I was confident that Mr. Taylor would be released.

CONSTATIN

I was sitting at my desk, watching my wife on the cameras. She had been working so hard to redecorate our home the way she wanted that I had to make sure she was eating and staying hydrated. We had fallen into a routine. For the last few weeks, she would spend all day redecorating the house or handling errands until I came home from work. Most nights, when I came home, we would watch TV, have sex, and fall asleep. On the weekends, she would ride along with me while I handled business, and then we would stop by a restaurant to eat dinner before returning home.

My office door opened, and I looked up, expecting to see my brothers. When I saw Kofi instead, I knew there had to be a good reason for him to enter my office without knocking. He always knocked first.

"I got them!" he excitedly said.

"Them, them? Well, today just got a whole lot more interesting. How did you find them?"

He hesitated before taking a deep breath and replying.

"Well, technically, I didn't. I know what you are thinking. How do I know that the information I received is valid? They sent me photos of Elizabeth and Tom. Now, I know the next question you're gonna ask me is: 'Who all knows that we are looking for them?' And that is why I believe that whoever sent these pictures anonymously must be someone trustworthy."

I heard him out and leaned back in my chair to study him. He received pictures from somebody anonymously, but he trusted them without knowing who sent them.

He might not know for sure who sent them, but something told me that he had an idea.

"Who do you think sent them?" I asked outright.

"What I think doesn't matter because I can't prove it, and to be honest, I don't want to get involved."

Now I was really interested. He was trying to protect someone.

I stared at Kofi, and he stared back. I decided to drop it because if Kofi didn't want to get involved, it had to be for his safety.

"Tell me what you know."

She and Tom have been staying in a motel in Suwanee, Georgia. It is about an hour and twenty minutes away from here, and it's a really small town. It's one of those towns where everybody knows you by name."

"We can meet up at Alexandur's at nine," I replied, letting him know that all of us were going hunting.

"Yes, sir. See you then," he said.

"Emet!" I yelled to my security guard.

When he entered my office, I told him what I needed him to pick up for us tonight before dismissing him.

I stayed at work until a little after eight p.m. and left to drive over to my brother's place. I parked my car, got out, and walked to the front door. Roman opened it, surprising me. He left work early to handle something and didn't return. I thought I would beat him here. Roman turned around and walked to the living room, where Alexandur and Kofi were.

"We are going to do a simple snatch and go. I need time, and we have to do a complete disposal," I told them before turning around and walking back to the front door and out of it.

They all came out a few seconds later, got in the car with me, and I pulled off. Alexandur and Kofi conversed while Roman and I remained quiet for the whole drive to Suwanee.

The name of the motel they were staying at was Red Roof. That surprised me because Elizabeth only liked luxury and high class everything.

The town was like a desert when I drove through it. No one was outside. All the restaurants looked abandoned. It was not until we pulled into the seedy motel that I saw a couple of people walking around.

Staying there was a smart decision because I would have never thought she would come to a place like that. She must have been letting Tom make all their decisions. I parked in front of room fifty-eight.

Only Alexandur and I got out. Roman and Kofi stayed in case Elizabeth or Tom tried to run.

The motel had cheap, flimsy doors that I could kick one time and open, but Alexandur used one of his credit cards to jimmy the door. We walked into the room like we owned it and quickly closed the door. Elizabeth must have heard the door close because she jumped up in bed. Before she could scream, I put my hand over her mouth. Alexandur searched the room for Tom but shook his head when he couldn't find him.

Fuck. I wonder if whoever sent those photos tipped him off?

"Listen, because I am only going to say this once. If you scream, your father is dead. If you try to run, your father is dead. If you do anything but get up and follow us to the car and then get in the backseat, your father is dead. Do I make myself clear?"

She nodded her head up and down. I let her mouth go and waited until she got off the bed and slid her shoes on before walking out of the motel room. I got back into the driver's seat.

Elizabeth and Alexandur got into the back. She was crying, but she should have been praying to repent for her evil soul before I sent her to wherever the fuck people go when they die.

"Where is Tom?" I asked her when we made it to where I was able to pull back onto the interstate.

"Fuck you. I know you got him. You can't stand the fact that I found a real man, so you had to hurt me?" she cried.

She deserved an Oscar for her performance. It was so good I almost believed her until I remembered that I did not know what the hell she was talking about.

The drive back to Alexandur's house took almost half the time it took to make it to Suwanee. Emet's car and Mikey's car were both parked in the driveway. I parked in my normal spot and got out.

"He already back there?' I asked my security guards.

"Yes, sir," they replied.

After hearing what I wanted to hear, I walked around back to Alexandur's very own version of a kill room. After we lost our father, none of us felt right killing in the kill room at our parents' home anymore.

Elizabeth's father tried to fight to get loose when I walked inside. Emet had him tied up good to a metal chair.

"Daddy!" Elizabeth screamed when she saw her daddy.

Alexandur led her to the other metal chair and tied her up as well. Alexandur's monster had to be craving to come out, but tonight was personal.

I waited until Alexandur moved to take my gun out from under my suit jacket and send a bullet through the mayor's knee. He screamed out in pain, but nobody outside would hear him. The building was soundproof.

I lifted my gun and aimed it at Elizabeth's head.

"Tell me where Tom is?" I asked her again.

"Your sick ass probably already killed him! I know you got him. I smelled that disgusting ass cologne when I came back to the room earlier and noticed Tom missing. You knew you couldn't fight a real man, you fucking psycho. I heard you had to pay a woman to marry you. You are nothing but a fucking failure who couldn't find anybody who wanted to be with you organically!" she yelled.

My right eye twitched. I turned around and shot her father in the stomach. She screamed and tried to fight against the rope holding her. I shot him three more times. The last one I put through the center of his forehead, killing him. She killed my father in front of me, and now we were even.

Well, not really. I emptied the rest of my bullets into her face. When I finished, I still didn't feel like we were even, but there were some things that I just had no control over. I slid my gun back into my jacket and dug my nails into my skin. We chopped their bodies up and watched them burn.

On the way home, I could not get her words out of my head. I pulled my phone out and texted Emet. Tonight was going to be a tough one. I prayed that I would be able to control myself.

Ari

Me: I think I love my husband

Kenya: I think you do, too

Me: Girl, bye. You swear you know me so bad!

Kenya: I do. Are y'all settled in?

Me: Yes, it took us a whole month, but all the major stuff is done now. It's going to take me at least another month to add all the minor things I want to each room. But I am happy to be back in the mansion.

Kenya: Don't overwork yourself. When we talked yesterday, you sounded terrible.

Me: Yeah, I think I was just exhausted because I feel much better today. Constatin just got home, though. I got to go. Love you.

I put my phone down and laid my head against my pillow. For the last couple of days, I had been throwing up. I figured it was because of the stress of moving until last night when I was arranging my and Constatin's his and hers bathroom.

I pulled out my box of tampons to put them away and noticed that the box wasn't open. That's when I realized I hadn't had my period this month. Instead of freaking out, I grabbed my phone to check the period tracker app I used every month, and I froze.

My period was eight days late. My period had never been late before. I bleed every twenty-eight days like clockwork. It was crazy because every time Constatin and I had sex, it was unprotected. I knew I would end up pregnant sooner or later. Now that the possibility of me being pregnant was staring me in the face, I didn't know how I felt about it.

Constatin and I have been doing good. We hadn't argued

since the gala last month. He had been making more time to spend with me, and we talked and texted frequently.

The only problem was that I was in love with him. Constatin has expressed that he has deep feelings for me, but there is a huge difference between having deep feelings for somebody and being in love with them. Tonight, when he got home, I planned to tell him that my period was late and admit that I was in love with him.

A crashing sound woke me up hours later. I yawned before sitting up in bed. It was dark outside my bedroom window, letting me know that I had been asleep for a while.

"Constatin?" I called out to my husband.

He didn't respond, but I could hear movement downstairs. Confused, I got up and slipped my house shoes on. On the stairs, I called Constatin's name again but again got no response. When I made it down the stairs, I had to turn on a few lights until I spotted my husband in the living room. He had blood on his clothes.

"Baby, are you okay?"

He didn't respond. In his hand was a glass cup with something brown inside it. He lifted the cup to his lips and took a sip.

"Constatin," I tried again.

"Leave," he finally answered.

"What do you mean leave? Leave and go where?"

He wasn't making any sense.

"Are you hurt?"

"I put a bullet in my best friend's head tonight for betraying me. No, I am not hurt. I want to hurt. I want to hurt so badly."

Elizabeth? Is he saying that he wants to hurt me or someone else? What in the entire fuck?

"Come on. Let me help you get cleaned up." I walked over to him, but when I reached to touch him, he pushed me away.

"Leave me the fuck alone. It's not safe. Go! Just fucking go! I don't want you around me!" he yelled.

This time, I listened. I slowly backed out of the living room. I heard another crashing sound, but I turned around and walked over to the staircase. My husband came stalking out of the living room, making my heartbeat race. He walked past me as if I were invisible and continued down the hallway. When he took a left, I knew he was going to his wine cellar, and that was still the one room that I was forbidden to enter.

Where the hell are Emet and Mikey?

I walked up the stairs and back to our bedroom. Confused, I thought about what had just happened. Did he want to hurt me, and why? Constatin had done a lot of fucked up shit to me, but I had never feared for my life like I did tonight.

What about the baby?

My hand went to my stomach, and I felt nauseous all over again. *What if he did hurt me? What if I am pregnant?*

Leave. He told you to leave.

I stood back up and grabbed my purse and keys. There was also extra security outside, but could they really stop me? Emet and Mikey would, in a heartbeat, but they weren't around.

My feet were moving before my brain could process what I was doing. I loved my husband, but I couldn't let him hurt me, and I damn sure wouldn't let him hurt my child if I was pregnant. When I made it to the front door, I paused and turned around to look at the home that I thought was mine.

If it's meant to be, it will be. Don't be a fool, though.

Constatin and I chose the security code for the alarm system together. It was the first three digits of his birthday and the first three digits of mine. I entered the alarm code and waited for the light to turn green.

Slowly, I stepped outside. It was pitch black out here. The walk to the security gate was a long one. When I approached it, I waved at the guard and pointed to the door. He frowned and picked up his phone to call somebody.

Fuck. My ass is about to die.

Whoever he called didn't answer because he tried to call again. Finally, he put the phone down and opened the gate. I waited until I made it out of the gate before I ordered an Uber to come and get me. When I got in the Uber, I told him to take me to the only place that I could think of.

Constatin

I woke up to my head killing me.

"Fuck," I muttered before rolling over and sitting up.

Slowly, I got up and rubbed my head. Last night was the worst it had ever gotten for me. Elizabeth's words triggered the shit out of me, and I spiraled out of control. Instead of harming myself, I drank myself to sleep. My phone vibrated in my suit pocket, and I pulled it out.

Emet: Are you okay?

Me: Yeah, you two can return.

Before I came home last night, I sent Emet and Mikey away. They were the only two who knew about my episodes, and the last time they tried to stop me, I almost killed them. That was almost six years ago, but I wasn't willing to test my limits last night.

I walked out of the wine cellar, and the house was quiet. Vaguely, I remembered my wife coming downstairs to check on me, but I sent her away.

"Ari!" I yelled her name while standing in the hallway.

Seconds passed before I ran up the stairs. A pain shot through my leg from running, but I did not stop until I reached our bedroom.

"*Regina mea* (my queen)," I said softly as I approached the bed.

Sooner or later, I will have to have a talk with her, I thought as I pulled the covers back. The bed was empty.

Where the fuck is my wife?

Dread filled my gut and spread throughout my whole body. I pulled my phone out and tried to call her phone, but it didn't ring. Confused, I tried again and got the same results. I dialed my brother's number, and the phone rang. When Alexandur answered, I hung up.

I pulled up the camera app on my phone and went to view what happened from one a.m. on. That was the last time frame that I remembered seeing on my phone before I started drinking. It was a little after two a.m. when I spotted her on the camera, turning on a light downstairs.

She walked into the living room and left back out six minutes later. I headed back down the stairs to check the living room while I watched the cameras. The living room was empty, but I sat down and continued watching the cameras until I spotted her leaving the house.

Emet and Mikey were pulling up when I walked out of the house. I opened the back door of Emet's car before he could get out and told him to take me to Alexandur's house.

On the ride over, I made a mental note to kill whichever security guard was on duty and let her out the fucking gate. Kofi and Roman's cars were parked at Alexandur's house. Hope filled my chest. I got out of the car and jogged up to my brother's door. It only took me a couple minutes to get the key out and unlock his door, but it felt like it took hours.

"ARI!" I yelled.

Noise was coming from the kitchen. I jogged into the kitchen and stopped when I spotted everybody but my fucking wife sitting at the table eating breakfast.

"Is Ari here?" I asked loudly, interrupting their conversation.

"No. Where is she supposed to be?" Kenya replied.

"Roman, please tell me the truth. Is my wife here?"

"You need to calm down. Have you looked into the mirror today?" Roman questioned, concerned.

I still had on yesterday's bloody clothes. I was supposed to burn everything when I got home, but I had already started to spiral.

I turned around and jogged up their stairs.

"ARI! ARI!" I yelled. My wife did not know anybody else. She had to be there.

I looked in every room. When I didn't find her, I jogged back down the stairs. Kofi was the only one still sitting at the table.

"Track my wife's phone."

"Okay, it won't take me long. How about you come have a seat? You are limping, and I don't want you to re-injure your leg," Kofi urged me.

My leg was hurting, but not more than the pain spreading in my chest. I hopped over to the kitchen table and sat down. Kofi began to type into his laptop. Seconds passed by slowly until he stopped typing to glance over at me.

"What?"

"Ummm... I can only track a number if it is in service. Her number is showing as disconnected."

My right eye started to twitch, and I felt my control slipping. "Are you saying that I failed my wife?"

"No, her phone might just be broken or something. Are you okay?"

Hurt. Hurt... HURT

Before I could stop myself, I reached into my suit and pulled my gun out.

"Oh, hell naw," Kofi muttered.

"Hurt. Hurt. Hurt." I rocked back and forth, muttering to myself.

My wife left me. I am a failure. I failed again and again and again.

I lifted the gun and smashed myself in the head repeatedly.

"Alexandur! Roman! Help now, hurry!" Kofi's voice yelled, but it sounded far away. Blood was oozing down my face, but I couldn't stop harming myself. I deserved to hurt.

Ari

I lay in bed and stared at the ceiling. My stomach growled, but I didn't want to get up. When I got here last night, the first thing I did was take the battery and the SIM card out of my phone. That wouldn't stop my husband from finding me, but I hoped it bought me a day or two until I had time to think.

I wanted to order a pregnancy test, but I didn't want to use my husband's card to do it. Why I didn't demand that he give me a lump sum of money, like he did my mother, was nothing but pure stupidity. I married a rich man and hadn't even thought once about the necessity of having my own money to use. It had to be some kind of mental illness.

I heard a knock, and then the door to my husband's old bedroom opened. His mother smiled at me warmly, and I smiled back at her.

"I made you some breakfast. Come eat," she softly said.

His mother's home was the only place that I could think of going without worrying about him finding out immediately. When her security called her and told her that I was there, she met me at the front door. The only thing she asked me was if he knew I was there, and I told her no.

"I'll be there in just a second," I replied.

She walked away from the room but left the door open. It took me another five minutes to get up, make his bed, and walk down the stairs. As soon as I entered the kitchen, the aroma of cooked food hit my nose, and I turned around and ran to the bathroom to throw up. When I finished, his mother was standing at the door with some toothpaste and a new toothbrush.

How can somebody so sweet push out something so evil?

"Thank you," I told her and took the items.

"Come back in here. I made you some soup and crackers," his mother yelled.

My stomach growled again, and I prayed I would be able to

keep the soup down. The aroma of whatever she had cooked was still in the air, but it wasn't strong. I sat down at the kitchen table, and she brought the soup and crackers and placed them in front of me. Cautiously, I scooped some of the soup up and sipped on it. It slipped down my throat, and I waited to see if it would try to come back up. When it didn't, I groaned and quickly ate the rest of the soup. His mother waited patiently for me to finish eating before she spoke.

"How late is your period?"

"Nine days, but I'm pretty sure I'm pregnant."

"Does he know?"

"No, but it is his fault that he doesn't."

"Do you love him?" she asked the million-dollar question.

Tears clouded my eyes, and I nodded my head 'yes' before crying my little eyes out.

Two nights later, I was lying in bed resting when I smelled him. The scent of his Baccarat cologne permeated the air around me, but I kept my eyes closed, pretending to still be asleep. I don't know how many minutes passed before he spoke.

"For two days, I have turned the whole world upside down, looking for you. And here you are, lying in my childhood bed, sleeping peacefully."

I opened my eyes and stared up into the complicated eyes of my husband. He looked terrible. An elastic bandage was wrapped around his head, and his eyes were bloodshot red as if he hadn't slept. He reached his left hand out and gently rubbed the back side of his hand across my cheek.

"Do you have nothing to say? Is this what you want? I told you over and over that I was not letting you go."

It sounded like he was threatening my life again, and I was just over it. At that point, death would be more welcoming than being in love with such a cold-hearted devil.

"Kill me or leave, but I'm done. You will not keep threatening to hurt me as if that shit is normal. I tried to make this work, and I do care about you so much, but this marriage is failing. So, either I'm taking my last breath tonight, or I'm filing for divorce," I told him.

His body moved back and forth in a swaying motion, and his right eye started twitching.

"I could never really hurt you, *regina mae* (my queen), but I can hurt me," he replied.

What?

Constatin looked me in the eyes, and I saw something shift. They looked sad and empty. He turned around and walked out of the room. I debated with myself for a minute before I got up and followed him. Constatin hadn't made it far down the stairs. He was walking slower than normal, but I still followed him at a safe distance. I watched him go into the kitchen, and I frowned, confused.

What the hell could he want to eat at this time of the morning? Lord, if I am walking to my death, haunt my husband for the rest of his life!

The light turned on in the kitchen. At a snail's pace, I continued to follow him. I turned into the kitchen behind him and then gasped.

Constatin was standing in the kitchen with a knife in his hand, cutting himself.

I*s that what he meant when he said he wanted to hurt? He was referring to himself?*

"Constatin, stop! Put the knife down!" I yelled at him.

He kept sawing the knife, slicing into the skin of his forearm from left to right and back again.

GOD! WHAT THE FUCK AM I SUPPOSED TO DO?!

"Seriously. Constatin, please stop," I pleaded with him.

"Leave. I need to hurt," he replied, his voice sounding like he was in a trance.

Without thinking, I grabbed a knife from the wooden knife block and sliced my arm with it, too.

Fuck, this shit hurts!

"Have you lost your fucking mind? What are you doing?" Constatin yelled at me.

"You put your knife down, and I will put mine down," I replied, trying hard not to show that I was in pain.

Constatin put his knife down and stalked toward me to snatch the knife out of my hand and then toss it in the sink. He had blood dripping all down his arm but was mad at my one little cut.

"Don't you ever do something so fucking stupid again. You do not hurt for me! I hurt for you."

"Or, how about both of us not hurt at all. Because every time you cut yourself, I am cutting myself too," I warned him.

Girl, you done lost your fucking mind.

"Why? I do not deserve you. You told me you wanted a divorce. Explain this to me, please. I do not understand." His voice had lowered, and he sounded hurt.

"Because I love you, Constatin. Why? I don't know because you are determined to drive me insane!"

Constatin looked at me in shock before lifting me off the ground and kissing me passionately. Neither of us cared that we were bleeding and getting it all over his mother's beautifully tiled kitchen floor.

"My life means nothing without you, Ari. Before I met you, my mind was in a constant gray state. From the time I was born, I began my training to become the Nasu and to take over my father's company. That's all I know. Whenever I failed, I had to punish myself because failure was not an option. Hurting myself has always been the only time I truly felt something inside until I met you. You own my heart. You control my dark soul. Without you, I am just gray matter."

"No more, Constatin. If I stay, you can not do this anymore. It is also not just about us anymore because I think I am pregnant."

Constatin gasped before falling to his knees in front of me

and kissing my stomach through my shirt multiple times. He then wrapped his arms around my waist and held me tight.

We stayed like that until his mother walked into the kitchen. Her eyes immediately zoomed in on the blood and cuts on our arms.

Epilogue
ARI

Four months later

Submit. I had an assignment due at midnight, but today was going to be a long day, so I got up early and got it done. If a black woman don't do anything else, we are going to get us some degrees. I was currently taking online classes for my master's in nursing. When I graduate, my husband would buy me my own practice as a graduation gift.

I had more than enough money in the bank to purchase my own small practice, but my husband would lose his shit. I turned my computer off and stood up to leave my office. My office, as I called it, was really just the bedroom next door to our bedroom. I had everything taken out and redecorated it with all the tools I would need to help me graduate in a year and a half.

When I walked into our bedroom, my reflection in the mirror caught my eye. My stomach was flat for the first few months of my pregnancy, and then one day, I just woke up with a baby belly. The bigger my stomach grew, the more reality sunk in that I really was about to be someone's mother. Today, I turned twenty weeks, and we were learning the gender at my doctor's appointment later.

Where in the hell is my husband?

My thoughts drifted to Constatin, and I smiled. Our marriage had blossomed so much over the last four months. After he found out about my pregnancy, he started getting psychiatric help from a woman who was nothing short of heaven-sent. A lot of her clients were criminals, which was why she was in such high demand. From what I heard, her estranged father was in the mafia. That is why she decided to help the people who had backgrounds tied to criminal organizations, but who knew if that was really true?

Her methods could sometimes be unorthodox, and they varied depending on the client. In Constatin's case, she focused heavily on healing his childhood trauma. He was born with such a great deal of pressure on his shoulders that he didn't allow himself to be a normal child like other kids did.

"Ari!" Constatin yelled my name from downstairs.

Speaking of the devil...

"Here I come!" I yelled back before giving myself one more glance in the mirror. Then, I picked up my purse and walked down the stairs. To my surprise, my husband wasn't standing at the bottom of the stairs as he usually would be. The only person I saw was Emet standing outside the kitchen.

I told him that he acts like he is the pregnant one because all he does is eat!

"Baby," I called out to him when I entered the kitchen. He was talking to two people with his back turned to me.

Hmmm... my husband wasn't big on handling his other business in the house.

Confused, I got closer and then stopped.

Is that my mommy?

My mommy gave me a smile but continued talking to my husband and whoever the man was standing in front of him. The man was tall, he and Constatin were almost the same height, and he had a bald head.

Who the hell is he? And why is everyone acting like I'm not the most important person in the room?

"HELLO!" I yelled.

"I told you she got a temper. I do not know why you insist on calling her your baby girl," I heard my husband say to the man and laugh.

Before I could cuss his ass out for talking about me to strangers, he turned around and moved to the side.

Oh, my God! Please, God. Don't let this be some kind of trick

Staring back at me was the man who always protected me, the one who saved my life, my own personal superhero.

I burst out crying like a big ass toddler.

"I told you she was going to do that, too. Our baby has her emotions all over the place," Constatin tried to whisper to my daddy, but I heard him.

One minute, my daddy and I were just staring at each other, and the next, I was in his arms. I hadn't felt my daddy's arms around me in over ten years, and the child inside me didn't want him to let go. Small arms wrapped around the other side of me. I knew my momma's touch from anywhere. All three of us embraced each other until my mother stepped away.

"We can hug some more later. Right now, I want to know what my first grandbaby is."

My father and I laughed, but he eventually stepped back. My handsome husband was standing there patiently, letting me have my moment.

"How did you do this?" I asked him.

"For you, there is not anything I wouldn't do. The day you told me what happened, I had Kofi pull his files, and the rest is history. He is a free man, and his murder charge has been dropped from his record."

Mentally, I made a note to give Kofi a big kiss on his cheek. He was always working hard for our family.

My husband reached out to grab my hand and lead me out of

the kitchen. My parents followed us. Mikey bought himself a new Ford Excursion when he found out I was pregnant.

He and Emet had both been arguing over who would be the baby's godfather. My name was Bennet, and I wasn't in it. That was a decision between my husband and them. My husband opened the door for me and helped me into the car, and then did the same for my parents.

The doctor's office parking lot was empty when we pulled into it. My psychotic husband didn't like to wait to have his child checked on, so he would pay for the doctor's office to be closed during my appointment times.

Mikey parked his Excursion and then got out to open the doors for everyone. Emet pulled in behind us and parked beside Mikey. We had to stay and wait for Emet to go inside the doctor's office and check each room. When Emet came out and told us everything was clear, we entered the doctor's office waiting area and were immediately taken to ultrasound.

The ultrasound tech helped me climb onto the exam table and told me to lift my shirt. My hand shook as I did what she asked. She opened the lip of a white tub of gel and applied the clear blue liquid over my entire stomach before placing the ultrasound wand on it. We all looked up at the ultrasound monitor to see that the baby was curled up, sucking on his or her thumb.

"Are you guys excited to find out what you're having?" the ultrasound lady asked.

"Excited is an understatement," I replied. In all honesty, it didn't matter to me if I was having a boy or a girl. I promised to protect my child and love him/her with every inch of my heart, regardless of what gender I have.

The lady moved the ultrasound wand around my stomach a few more times before pressing down in one spot. She squinted and smiled.

"Congratulations! It looks like y'all are having a boy!"

My husband, who had been quiet the entire time, was now

cheering like his favorite football team had just won the Superbowl.

My father reached over and gave him a hug. I couldn't wait to hear the details behind my father's release because he and my husband were too comfortable with each other to have just met personally.

The ultrasound tech spent a couple more minutes taking pictures of the baby before she used a paper towel to wipe the cool gel off my stomach. She helped me back down off the exam table, and we were escorted out into the doctor's main office.

We didn't stay inside her office for long. She measured my belly and then told me everything looked fine and to come back next month. My husband was trying to convince me to have a natural birth like his mother did, but I politely told him that he could kiss my entire natural black ass.

Speaking of his mother, when we got back in the Excursion, that is where we headed. The relationship between her and me continued to grow after everything that had happened since the night I popped up on her doorstep.

Today, she was cooking me a big feast to celebrate learning the gender of her grandbaby. I was so happy that she was getting the chance to meet my parents. I believed they all would get along nicely.

When we pulled into his mother's driveway, Roman, Alexandur, and Kenya were already there. As soon as we walked through the door, my best friend and her small baby bump were waiting. Kenya and I agreed that every time one of us got pregnant, the other would, too. That way, all our kids would be close in age and become best friends, like her and I.

She wouldn't find out what she was having until next month, but I was the one hosting her gender reveal party. Kenya led me to the dining room, where everyone was. When I walked inside, everybody cheered. There were balloons hanging up and baby decorations everywhere.

In that moment, my heart had never felt so full. I glanced

around the room at all the people I had grown to love and felt immensely blessed. My love story was an unconventional one. It was not one with softness and light. No, my love story was one full of darkness and pain. And I would do it all over again in a heartbeat.

Roman

I leaned back in the corner and watched my family as they celebrated the future birth of my nephew. Mom had gone all out, cooking and baking a lot of traditional Romanian and American dishes. I wished my father was still alive. He would have been so happy to learn that Constatin was having a boy. Some of his happiness would have been for unethical reasons, but nonetheless, it would have made him happy. From the corner of my eye, I watched as my older brother approached me.

Hmmmm... he looks serious.

He stood in front of me and stared at me, but I kept my expression blank and waited for him to tell me whatever had brought him into my personal space.

"I know you have been running around here, killing people and setting their bodies on fire. And before you try to deny it, I followed you yesterday and watched you kill a person with your bare hands and set them on fire. Now, last time I checked, the mafia did not have any current problems that needed to be resolved. That worries me.

"Tonight, I decided to be your big brother when I approached you instead of your Nasu. As your big brother, I feel like I was not there for you when Father passed like I should have been. This is me making it up to you. Constatin reached into his pocket, pulled out a black card, and handed it to me. On the card were the words, "Brittany Gabriellei. Psychiatrist," and nothing else.

Was he sending me to a psychiatrist? What the fuck!

"In my heart, I am hoping that you are killing as a result of PTSD and not because you just want to be a serial killer."

We all kill people, stupid.

"Your first appointment is scheduled for Monday at 9:00 p.m. Roman, you will attend these appointments every week, and you will continue to attend until she feels like you're healed. Now, that is a direct order from your *Nasu*." Constatin reached his hands out and tried to hug me. I just stared at him until he dropped his arms and walked away.

I stayed in the same corner for another ten minutes until the itch became unbearable. Without saying a word to anybody but my mother, I left. My home was only twenty minutes away. I only had two security guards who watched my home, and they were not allowed to be anywhere near the front door. Their only job was to protect the perimeter.

My father used to make me always walk around with two security guards until I kept killing them. After I killed the sixth or seventh one, he made up excuses to my brothers about me not needing them anymore because I had my brothers to protect me, and they believed him. I parked in my driveway and got out of my car.

The Itch was getting stronger. It was taking everything in me to walk calmly to my front door, unlock it, and enter. When I got in the house, I immediately walked to the back and down the stairs to my basement. Before I got to the bottom step, I could hear chains rattling.

"You miss me?" I asked Tom or what was left of him. Tom could not respond because he did not have his tongue or any teeth left in his mouth.

"You missed one hell of a satisfying meal. I know how you love my mother's cooking. I am so full; I feel like I could burst."

Tom made incomprehensible noises before crying. He had not eaten anything in four days now, and I knew he was starving. I walked over to my tray and picked up a scalpel before advancing toward him.

"Enough of the small talk. It's time to play," I said, grinning.

To be continued....

To my readers:
Thank you all so much. I appreciate each and every one of you. Please consider leaving me an honest review. It helps me out so much. I hope you all enjoyed the wild ride we had with Constatin and Ari. Constatin was the most complex character I have written so far, and I was stressed, lol. Roman and Britt's story is up next. It will also be an interracial dark romance, but it will be dark in a more sexual and funny way. To stay informed on all projects and sneak peeks, follow me on Facebook: Author Jatoria Crews, and join my author's group, Jatoria C. Book Cove. My IG, TikTok, and Threads are all under Author Jatoria Crews. All of this information above can be found on my website:www.author-jatoriac.com. Thank you again for the support.

Also by Jatoria C.

The Devil Wears Baccarat

Obsessed With A Plus Size Barbie 3

Obsessed With A Plus Size Barbie 2

Obsessed With A Plus Size Barbie

Alexa, Play I Need A Rich Thug Husband 2

Alexa, Play I Need A Rich Thug Husband